Wolfe was stark naked

Wendy froze, stu_____
_away. Leave_____
when her e_____
beautiful ma_____

Suddenly he b_____ y thought
about running, _____ saw her, and
she knew it was _____ As he turned and
sat up on the edg__ of the bed, for a split
second she was sure she was going to get a
glimpse of the part of his body that would
make the rest of him pale in comparison.

'What are you doing in here?'

She opened her mouth, but nothing came
out. Her eyes roved over his body as if they
had a mind of their own, finally landing below
his waist.

'Hey!' he said. 'You want to look somewhere
else? Pervert.'

Pervert? He was calling her a _pervert_?

'Exhibitionist,' she muttered.

'I live here! If you don't like it, you know
where the door is!'

'Actually,' she said, 'I like it just fine.'

Dear Reader,

Picture yourself the victim of a turn of events that leaves you stranded at midnight in the middle of a sleet storm on the mean streets of an unfamiliar city. You have no coat, no money and you know no one within five hundred miles.

Now imagine you hear the roar of an engine, and the biggest, baddest man you've ever seen rides up on a motorcycle. He offers to take you someplace warm and safe. What do you do? Keep walking and freeze to death, or hop on and hope for the best? That's the situation Wendy Jamison finds herself in, and the decision she makes changes her life!

Wendy Jamison and Michael Wolfe are as different as any two people can be, but it doesn't take long before she sees beyond his big, bad image and brings out the kind and compassionate man he really is. And little does she know that when he offers to let her stay with him for one night, there are going to be many more hot nights to come!

Visit me on the web at www.janesullivan.com, or write to me at jane@janesullivan.com. I'd love to hear from you!

Best wishes,

Jane Sullivan

TALL, DARK AND TEXAN

by

Jane Sullivan

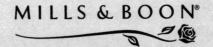

MILLS & BOON®

To all my wonderful friends at Dallas Area Romance Authors. You amuse me, amaze me and inspire me. Thanks for all the good times. I'm looking forward to many more!

First published in Great Britain 2005
by Harlequin Mills & Boon Limited,
Eton House, 18-24 Paradise Road, Richmond, Surrey TW9 1SR

© Jane Graves 2004

ISBN 0 263 84404 8

21-0205

Printed and bound in Spain
by Litografía Rosés S.A., Barcelona

1

WENDY JAMISON CREPT her 1992 Buick along the dark, deserted street, the February sleet storm pummeling her car and freezing wind whistling through the torn weather stripping around the passenger window. She hadn't planned on taking a midnight tour of the seedy part of downtown Dallas, but she'd lost track of the turns she'd made since exiting the freeway in search of a gas station and now she was hopelessly lost.

On either side of her, warehouses loomed several stories into the night sky, the majority of them boarded up. Most of the storefronts looked abandoned, topped by apartments that showed only an occasional dim light in a window. The sleet had stuck trash to the sidewalk in big, soggy piles that would probably still be there after the spring thaw. If it had been a hot summer night, the place would undoubtedly be crawling with the shadier side of society, but now, when she desperately needed to ask somebody how to get back to the freeway, there wasn't a pimp, a crack whore or a drug dealer in sight.

The problem was the trailer she was pulling. Filled with everything she owned, it had played hell with her mileage, running the little arrow on her gas gauge right into the red before she realized it. When that same little arrow had stopped floating and she still hadn't found an open station, she'd gotten a little uptight.

Now, ten minutes later, she was wiping her sweaty palms

on her jeans, trying to get a grip, telling herself that this was just one of those worst-case-scenario situations, which there had to be a solution to. Wendy knew how to stay alive during an avalanche, how to escape a sinking car and how to survive if her parachute failed to open in the event that she lost her mind and went skydiving. Unfortunately, she'd never read about how to get out of a sleazy, unfamiliar, convoluted downtown neighborhood during a winter storm in a car that was choking along on its last gas fumes.

Find a way. You'll never get to L.A. if you can't get through Dallas first.

She pulled up to the next intersection, which looked every bit as squalid as the last one. Putting her car in Park, she fumbled through the stuff on her passenger seat, looking for the Texas map she'd picked up at the border. She doubted it would include a map specific enough to get her back to the freeway, but right now it was her only shot.

Then she noticed movement outside her driver's window. Whipping around, she was shocked to see a man standing beside her car. A big, ugly, hairy man.

A big, ugly, hairy man holding a baseball bat.

In the next instant, her car window exploded. She shied away, throwing up her arms against the sudden blast of broken glass. In the time it took her to realize that he'd whacked the baseball bat right through her window, he'd reached in, pulled up the door lock and yanked her door open. The moment he grabbed her arm, though, self-preservation kicked in. She remembered the mantra she'd learned during the two-hour crash course on self-defense she'd taken at a New York YMCA: *Get mad, get loud, get violent.*

Letting out a nerve-shattering scream, she swung her foot out of the car and gave her attacker a boot right in the knee. He drew back, retaliating with an arm-wrenching yank that pulled her halfway out of the car. When she reached for the steering wheel and held on tightly, he leaned into the car to pry her fingers loose.

Everything's a weapon, her German Amazon-woman instructor had said. *Use whatever you've got.*

With a fury that would have made Greta proud, Wendy bit her attacker's hand. He recoiled, howling with pain, but before she could turn and get in another well-placed kick, he gave her arm a brutal jerk that dislodged her grip from the steering wheel. The next thing she knew, she was face-down on the slush-covered pavement.

She pushed herself back up and flipped over, rocking to a squatting position, but he'd already slid into the front seat. Her car wasn't much, and neither were her possessions, but the five thousand dollars in her glove compartment was something she had no intention of giving up.

With a desperate lunge, she grabbed the foot he hadn't yet tucked inside the car. The second she clamped down on it, he shook it wildly, but she clung to it like a bulldog.

"Damn it, lady!" he shouted. "Will you cut that out?"

"No! *You're not taking my car!*"

"Oh, yeah? Is that right?"

He reached beneath his coat, hauled out a gun and leveled it three inches from her nose.

Uh-oh.

She stopped pulling on his leg and stared down the barrel of the gun, breathing hard, wondering why her life wasn't flashing before her eyes.

"Let go!" he shouted.

She did.

"Back off!"

As she leaned away, her heel slipped from beneath her and her butt landed on the slushy pavement. Her friendly neighborhood carjacker slammed the door, jammed the car into gear, gunned the engine and took off down the street.

Wendy scrambled to her feet, watching her car vanish into the night, willing it to use up its last trickle of gasoline and come to a choking halt.

It didn't.

She stood there dumbly for a moment, staring at her red taillights twinkling through the falling ice. She couldn't believe she'd been in town only twenty minutes, and already she was a crime statistic. She couldn't believe everything she owned in the entire world had just disappeared. She couldn't believe she was standing in the disgusting part of downtown Dallas at midnight with no coat and it was thirty degrees and sleeting like crazy and *her car had just been stolen!*

Along with her five thousand dollars.

A sick feeling rose in her stomach. It was gone. And she wasn't naive enough to think she'd ever see it again. She knew the time would come when she'd probably sob uncontrollably about that, but right now she had a much bigger problem.

Survival.

Anger had kept her momentarily oblivious to the cold, but now reality set in. She hugged herself, her teeth chattering so hard it had to be knocking her fillings loose. The frigid wind seemed to blow right through her, echoing through the empty streets like the mournful howl of a coyote, and she wondered how long she could last out here before hypothermia set in.

She started to walk, chastising herself with every step. If only she hadn't gotten impatient, she could have waited out the winter storm of the decade and stayed on course through Oklahoma City instead of swinging south through Dallas. If only she hadn't messed around finding a gas station, she'd be in a cheap but warm hotel room right now. If only the windows of her old Buick were as strong as the Popemobile's—

Stop with the ifs. Things happen. This is just one of them. A speed bump on the road of life.

Actually, it was more like a speed *mountain*, one she'd have preferred to hit while driving through Miami. She made a mental note that the next time she decided to move across the country and start a new life, she'd wait until July.

She trudged down the sidewalk, every muscle trembling in the cold, her boots slinging slush. Putting a hand to her head, she realized that her hair was turning into icicles. The longer she walked, the more uptight she became. This street seemed to be going nowhere. For all she knew, she could be walking straight into hell.

Then again, at least hell would be warm.

Then she heard it. The sound of an engine. It was soft at first, building in intensity as it drew closer, echoing off the walls of the abandoned buildings. She turned around to see a man on a motorcycle swing around and come to a halt in the street ten feet away, planting his booted feet firmly on the pavement. The moment she laid eyes on him, her breath caught in her throat.

He wore a fleece-lined black leather jacket, jeans, black gloves, black boots. Even sitting on the motorcycle, she could tell he had to be at least six foot five, with thighs the size of tree trunks and shoulders so broad she wondered if he could clear the average doorway. A jagged scar ran from his cheekbone to his chin, the kind men generally picked up in street fights or in prison, but his dark, short-cropped hair and surprisingly clean-shaven face made him seem almost handsome in spite of it.

No. She was seeing things. This man was not handsome. No man who wore that tense, almost lethal expression, with eyes that could burn holes through steel, could ever be called handsome.

Still…good *Lord*.

In spite of the situation, in spite of the cold, in spite of the fact this man radiated *danger* all over the place, a blast of raw sexual awareness overwhelmed her, a prehistoric reaction that even a million years of evolution couldn't possibly arrest. She'd heard once that power was the ultimate aphrodisiac, and this man exuded it with every breath he took.

He leveled a gaze at her that would have frozen her to the pavement if nature hadn't beaten him to it. "What are you doing out here?"

His voice was deep and commanding—the voice of a man who expected an answer the moment he spoke.

"I—I was carjacked," she said, her voice garbled from the cold. "They got everything."

"Live here, or just passing through?"

"Heading to L.A."

"Do you know anybody in Dallas?"

"N-no," she said. "Nobody."

For the first time, his intense expression shifted. He bowed his head, his body heaving with a sigh.

"Get on," he said.

She blinked with surprise. "E-excuse me?"

"I said get on."

Get on? Behind him? A clearly unhappy man who looked as if he ate scrap metal for breakfast? It was one thing to admire the king of beasts from afar, but she wasn't sure she should be crawling right into the cage with him.

"Uh…sure. Can you take me to the police station?"

"Not tonight. Too far away, and it's too damned cold. I'll take you someplace warm and safe."

Warmth and safety. Currently the two most beautiful

concepts in the English language. But was this the man who was going to provide those things?

She looked around, shivering wildly, looking for options and finding none.

He revved the engine. Last call.

She mentally crossed herself, strode over and slung her leg over the back of his motorcycle.

"Hang on, sweetheart."

He hit the throttle, and only by clamping her arms around his waist was she able to keep from tumbling off backward. And in spite of the cold, the noise of the engine and her massive fear of the unknown, her only thought was that she'd just grabbed the Rock of Gibraltar. Even through the thick jacket he wore, she could tell he was all bone and muscle.

"Where exactly are we going?" she shouted.

No response. Either he couldn't hear her over the roar of the engine, or he chose to ignore her. As they sped down the deserted street, her icy hair swirled in a frenzy around her head, the frigid strands smacking her in the face. She ducked her head against his back, hoping to keep the ice cubes that had once been her ears from cracking and falling off the sides of her head. He made an excellent wind block, which was no surprise. A man his size could have blocked a category-five hurricane. Even through his jacket she could feel his body heat, and right now, heat from anywhere was welcome. She closed her eyes, resurrected a few childhood prayers and hung on tight.

He seemed to drive forever before finally slowing down, and as soon as he did, he reached into his pocket and pulled out something that looked like a television remote. He pointed it at a large metal overhead door on the side of one of the buildings. With a grinding mechanical noise, the door came up. To her complete shock, he drove right underneath

it into the building, the engine noise of the motorcycle reverberating off the walls of the empty warehouse.

She glanced over her shoulder to see the door coming
down behind them. That familiar sense of self-preservation
surged through her again, but Greta hadn't addressed what
do to when trapped on a moving vehicle behind a man the
size of a redwood tree.

"Hey!" she shouted. "Where are you going? Hey!"

He never slowed down. He continued through the musty-
smelling warehouse, dimly lit by a few overhead bulbs.
Twenty feet in the distance stood two large metal doors. He
leveled the remote at them, and they parted just as he
reached them. He drove between them and swung the motorcycle around in a tight one-eighty just as the doors closed
again. She looked around to see that they'd entered a room
the size of a small bedroom. No doors, no windows. Then
she heard a creaking noise, and it began to move.

Good God, they were on an elevator.

"Where are you taking me?" she asked as they slowly ascended, her voice still paralyzed by the cold.

"Home," he said.

"Whose home?"

"Mine."

He lived here? What could possibly live in a place like this
besides rats, roaches and ghosts?

Serial killers.

Live here, or just passing through? he'd asked her. *Know anybody in Dallas?* He might as well have said, *Hop on, baby. It's
easier to get away with murder if you're a transient.*

No. He'd said warm and safe. She'd heard him very
clearly. It might have been a big fat lie, but right now she
had no choice but to pray he was telling her the truth.

The elevator chugged up three floors and stopped. The
doors creaked open in concert with the soft rumble of the

idling engine. He eased the motorcycle forward until it exited the elevator, then killed the engine.

Wendy instantly got off and backed away. The light was dim, but still she could tell they were standing on a large three-story-high platform enclosed by an iron railing. The elevator led to one place—to this landing and a large metal door dead ahead.

He smacked the kickstand down with his foot, got off the bike and stepped toward the door. Behind her, the elevator doors screeched closed. She whipped around, looking to the left of the elevator, then to the right. Where was the control panel?

"Uh...no buttons," she said. "How do you call the elevator?"

He held up the remote, then stuffed it into his coat pocket.

"Stairwell?"

"Not out here."

She was trapped.

She backed against the iron railing, her heart racing wildly, her teeth still chattering like crazy, sounding like a jackhammer in the silence of the huge warehouse.

The man slipped his gloves off, stuffed them into his hip pocket, then pulled out a set of keys. He unlocked one lock. Then another. After the turn of a third key, he swung the door open, stepped aside and nodded for her to enter the darkened room.

He'd looked big sitting on the motorcycle. He looked positively gigantic now. Her question of whether he could make it through a doorway with those shoulders was answered.

Barely.

Swallowing hard, Wendy glanced back at the useless elevator. The nonexistent stairwell. The sheer three-story drop over the railing. She wished she had a choice, but the weather, the situation and the look on this man's face had relieved her of all of those. Taking a deep, shaky breath, she walked through the door into the darkened room.

Okay. It's warm in here. At least he didn't lie about that.

That was her first thought, and for several heavenly seconds, it was her only thought.

Then he turned on the lights.

2

WENDY BLINKED against the sudden brightness, shocked at what came into view. The room was massive. No, it wasn't a room. Just an extension of the warehouse that contained it, with soaring ceilings crisscrossed with pipes and ducts and wires. Along one wall was a refrigerator, a stove and a few cabinets, with a nearby table and a couple of chairs, which she guessed qualified that area as the kitchen.

Near an adjoining wall sat a television with a sofa in front of it. Against another wall was a desk with a phone, computer monitor, scanner, fax machine, printer. Industrial light fixtures hung from the ceiling, illuminating the room with a garish glow. The floor was nothing more than cracked, stained concrete without a rug in sight.

She heard a clanking noise. Turning back, she saw him lock the door with twists, swipes and flips of his fingers. "Stay here," he commanded, then disappeared down a short hallway into another room.

Wendy looked around the bizarre warehouse loft. The furniture, the computer equipment and the TV should have made it seem at least a little homey, but stuck inside this weird place, they looked strange and surreal. And not a single personal item graced a shelf, table or kitchen counter to indicate that he was a normal human being and not a reclusive psychopath. She tried desperately to get a grip on herself, but in spite of the warmth of the room, fear mingled with the cold she still felt until she couldn't tell which one was making her shiver.

Venturing forward, she peered around a corner into another area and saw a door standing slightly open. A moment later she heard a scratching noise, and the door creaked open a few inches more.

When a cat the size of a Yugo sauntered out of the room, Wendy leaped back with surprise. The animal stopped suddenly and glowered at her, and she was sure she'd never seen a more wicked-looking feline. He had fire-orange stripes, scruffy fur and paws the size of boxing gloves. But the scariest thing of all were his appendages, or lack of them. All of his left ear and half of his tail were missing.

Good God. He's eating the cat. One bite at a time.

And now the cat was going to eat her.

"Hey, kitty-kitty," she said in her best cat-whisperer voice. "Nice kitty."

The creature tensed. Then all at once he hissed, scurried across the floor, leaped to the kitchen counter and then to the top of the refrigerator, where he glared down at her with evil yellow eyes. Wendy backed up to the wall, her hand against her chest, trying to calm her wildly beating heart. It couldn't get any creepier here. No way could it get any creepier.

Then she looked toward the room from which the cat had just emerged.

Maybe it could.

With a compulsion she couldn't quell, Wendy tiptoed over and pushed the door open just enough that she could see what was on the other side, and anxiety surged through her all over again.

On a table lay three guns. She didn't know a derringer from an Uzi, but she certainly knew a firearm when she saw one.

Then she looked up on the wall.

At least forty photographs were stuck there. They appeared to be mug shots—mug shots of men who were mean and nasty looking, like particularly despicable serial killers. And through about half of the photos were big black Xs. He was marking them out, one by one, with a supersize Magic Marker, as if...

As if he'd *snuffed* them.

Then it struck her. *He's a serial killer who kills serial killers.* Did it get any badder than that?

She quickly pulled the door closed and turned around. She could hear her captor knocking around in the other room, undoubtedly getting the torture chamber ready.

She had to get out of there.

Turning, she spied another door beside the refrigerator, one with as many locks as had been on the front door. He'd told her there wasn't a stairwell in the elevator landing. Maybe that door led to one. She hoped it did, anyway, because otherwise there was no getting out of this apartment.

No. Not apartment. More like lair. Or hideout. Or fortress. Or covert base of operations. What in the hell did you call a place that looked more like a bunker than living quarters?

A place she wanted to escape. Right now.

She hurried toward the door, looking over her shoulder, watching for him to come out of the back room. As quietly as she could, she opened the first dead bolt, which made a hideous clanking noise. Then she unhooked a chain that had links as wide as her wrist. She was just about to push a heavy metal slide lock aside when she heard footsteps. Spinning around, she saw him walking toward her. With a quick, startled breath, she pressed her back against the door.

"Where are you going?" he demanded.

Fueled by sheer adrenaline, she wheeled back around, smacked the last lock and yanked the door open. Just as quickly, he took a few steps forward and grabbed her from behind, wrapping his arm around her waist and pulling her back as he shut the door again. She screamed, a hair-raising, penetrating scream that could easily have awakened any dead bodies he happened to have lying around. He slapped his hand over her mouth, shoving her scream all the way back into her throat. She tried to fight him, but he pressed his body hard to hers, pinning her against the door.

"Will you cut it out?" he said. "You're not going anywhere!"

She couldn't struggle anymore. With a ton of bone and muscle wrapped around her, she was completely at his mercy.

"I'm going to take my hand away from your mouth," he said, his voice low and intense. "Are you going to scream?"

She just stood there, terrified.

"I asked you if you're going to scream," he said sharply.

Finally she shook her head. He removed his hand slowly, and her breath came in sharp bursts that seemed to echo forever in the vast expanse of the warehouse.

"If you're going to do this," she said in a hushed voice, "then do it now. Get it over with quickly. Please."

He froze. "If I'm going to do what?"

She closed her eyes. "Rape me. Kill me. Whatever...whatever it is you do."

For a count of three, he stood motionless. "What did you say?"

She didn't want to repeat it. She'd barely been able to get the words out the first time. "R-rape me. And kill—"

Suddenly he let go of her. She spun around, her back pressed to the door, breathing hard. He'd retreated several paces, staring at her with disbelief. "What in the *hell* are you talking about?"

She swallowed hard. "If you're not going to hurt me, then why are you trying to stop me from leaving?"

"Why am I—?" He stopped short, staring at her as if she'd lost her mind. He pointed toward the window. "Is it thirty degrees out there? Sleeting?"

She looked over at the ice still pattering the window. "Uh...yeah."

"Are there lowlifes wandering the streets?"

Clearly there were. One of them had made off with her car. "A few."

"Do you have any idea at all where you are?"

Hell, no. A global-positioning system couldn't have helped her out of here. She shrugged. "No. I guess I'm not completely sure."

"Those are three real good reasons. One would have done just fine. But if you're still determined to leave," he said, his voice a low growl, "there's a police station about four miles west. Why don't you hike on down there and tell them there's a rapist on the loose?"

She blinked with surprise, startled at this turn of events. Although he was rumbling with anger, she noticed that his dark eyes didn't seem nearly as evil as they had a few moments ago. Actually, they looked more sleepy than anything. And he'd made a couple of pretty good points about the weather and all those other things.

Was it possible she could have leaped to a conclusion or two?

"Okay," she said, shrugging weakly, "so maybe you're not a criminal."

"Hell, no, I'm not!"

She recoiled at his angry outburst. "Hey! What was I supposed to think? The abandoned warehouse, the guns, the mug shots, the big black *X*s—"

"You saw all that? What were you doing in there?"

"I—" She stopped, then pointed to the cat on top of the fridge. "He opened the door. I just...I just kinda looked in."

"You were snooping?"

Her mouth fell open. "I was *not* snooping! I was just trying to find out what kind of fire I landed in when I fell out of the frying pan!"

His eyebrows flew up. "Fire? Are you kidding? I bring you someplace warm where you can stay the night, then keep you from running back out there again like some kind of lunatic, and you call that a *fire?*"

She opened her mouth to respond, then clamped it shut again. He was making more sense all the time.

She nodded toward the other room. "What about the guns you have in there?"

He glared at her. "Those weapons are for my job."

"Your job?"

"I'm a bail-enforcement agent."

"Huh?"

"Bounty hunter."

Bounty hunter?

It took a full ten seconds for the words to register in Wendy's mind, and when they did, relief swooped through her. The guns, the mug shots...okay. Maybe those made sense now. It still didn't explain the living accommodations and the half-eaten cat, but...

"You go after criminals?" she asked him.

"Yes."

"Bad guys?"

"Yes."

She peered up at him. "Which means you can't *be* a bad guy...right?"

"I already told you I'm not a bad guy!"

She flinched. "Oh, come on! What else was I supposed to think? Don't you think that any sane woman would have come to the same conclusion I did? That you just *might* be a little dangerous?"

"Dangerous?"

"Yes! Will you look at yourself, for heaven's sake? You're big, you're scary looking, and I'm pretty sure you could bite the head right off somebody's shoulders if you wanted to. That doesn't give me a lot of warm fuzzies, you know."

He blinked and, for a moment, looked surprised. Maybe even a little insulted. Then just as quickly, his expression melted back into the scowl he'd been wearing before.

"Listen, sweetheart. It's late, I'm tired and I'm fresh out of warm fuzzies. Sleep on the sofa if you want, leave if you want. I don't give a damn."

Taking a key from his pocket, he strode over to the door to the war room, pulled it shut and locked it. He disappeared down the hall, turning into what she guessed must be a bedroom.

Then...silence.

Wendy stood there, shivering, swearing she could hear the sound of his angry voice still echoing through the vast expanse of the warehouse loft. Well, she had news for him. He couldn't be fresh out of warm fuzzies, because he'd never had any to begin with. He'd scared the hell out of her, then acted as if it was her fault.

A bounty hunter. As if she would have guessed that? Ever?

With a few deep, calming breaths, her heart rate slowly returned to normal. At least now she knew she'd live to be broke and homeless another day. And unless she committed a crime and jumped bail, her big, angry roommate probably wasn't going to be a threat. For tonight, at least, she had a place to stay that wasn't a cardboard box on the streets of downtown Dallas.

Then she turned, and for the first time, she noticed two

blankets and a pillow tossed on the sofa that hadn't been there before. She stared at them oddly for a moment, wondering where they'd come from.

Then she knew. He had to have brought them out of the bedroom while she was trying to make her escape. She walked over and picked up one blanket, catching the scent of something soft and fresh. Drawing it to her nose, she inhaled. Fabric softener?

Then she saw the shirt.

Sticking out from beneath the pillow was a green flannel shirt. She held it in front of her. From the size of it, she knew it had to be his. She blinked at it dumbly for a moment before the reason he'd left it here finally dawned on her.

He was giving her something dry to put on.

She pulled the shirt against her nose and smelled the same fresh fabric softener. She could wrap herself in it three times over, but it felt so warm...

He was trying to be nice, and she'd called him a criminal. A couple of different kinds of criminal, in fact.

Suddenly she felt bad about that. No, he hadn't told her exactly who he was, but it had been cold and sleeting, and not knowing how long she'd been out there, maybe he'd just wanted to get her warm again as quickly as he could. The blankets and the flannel shirt attested to that.

Now she felt worse than bad.

She glanced toward the room he'd disappeared into, her stomach churning with regret. She thought about knocking on his door to say she was sorry, but with her rapist-murderer accusation still rattling around inside his head, she didn't think he'd want to hear anything from her right about now. Tomorrow morning might be a better time for apologies.

She went over to the wall and flicked out the light. By the faint glow of a streetlamp coming in through metal casement windows, she scurried back to the sofa, quickly peeled off her wet clothes and slipped into the shirt. It hung all the way to her knees, but what a feeling. Warmth.

She tossed the pillow at one end of the sofa, then spread out the blankets. She laid her wet clothes over a chair in the kitchen area and eased down on the sofa, tucking herself beneath the blankets.

In spite of the weird situation, she found her thoughts drifting to the man in the other room. He might have been big and scary and all those other things, but as she played the past half hour over in her mind, she realized that a knight on a white horse couldn't have done a better job of rescuing her.

Yes, she thought sleepily. She had to tell him she was sorry. He deserved it. And on the selfish side, an apology might keep him from kicking her out the door first thing tomorrow morning before she had a chance to get her bearings.

Right now, her situation looked a little scary. Okay, a lot scary. She had no money, no car, no clothes. Nothing but the wallet in her pocket, which held maybe five bucks and zero credit cards. But she always landed on her feet, and this time wouldn't be any different. That was what she told herself, anyway, to keep from bursting into tears.

You can't do this. You've hit a dead end. Go home.

In the next instant, she slapped herself for that thought. She didn't care if she had one foot dangling over a cliff with a seventy-mile-per-hour tailwind, she was going to hang on by her fingernails if that was what it took. Aside from her once-a-year holiday trips to see her family, she had no intention of going back to obscurity again. She thought about the factory where she'd worked for four years alongside her parents, her eight siblings and just about every other resident of Glenover, Iowa. It was just what you did when you graduated from high school. A regular paycheck. Sick days. Job security. *Yuck.*

She'd had bigger dreams.

When she was a senior in high school, she'd starred in Glenover High's productions of *Our Town* and *Bye, Bye Birdie,* and for the first time in her life, she felt truly special. Raised in such a large family, the spotlight rarely made its way around to her, so those few magical nights had been intoxicating.

For the next four years, the thrill of it stayed in the back of her mind, until finally she couldn't stand it any longer. She left behind the dreary, monotonous, unremarkable town where she'd been raised and headed for the bright lights of the New York stage, knowing in her heart that she was destined to become a star.

Three years, six dead-end jobs and eighty-seven auditions later, she realized she'd made a small miscalculation. In New York, they expected superior craft and exceptional talent and years of paying dues, so actors built careers with the speed of glaciers melting. But in Hollywood...

Now, there was a place where a person could shoot to superstardom overnight. Life was too short to wait around. Once the lightbulb had gone on and she'd realized the error in her thinking, she'd felt compelled to move on as quickly as she could, determined to make something happen *now.*

Through a friend of a friend, she'd managed to hook up with an agent who'd promised he could get her the contacts she needed, and she knew how to make the most of them. Talent wasn't a list-topping requirement on the West Coast, so the fact that she was a pretty decent actress meant she was already ahead of the game. She had smarts, she had ambition and she had the right look. Or most of the right look, anyway. She could buy the rest of the appearance she needed just as soon as she found a way to get five thousand dollars back in her pocket again.

Wendy settled back on the pillow and closed her eyes, feeling exhausted right down to her bones. All she needed was a good night's sleep, some morning light on her face and a cup of coffee past her lips. Once her brain was working, she could formulate a plan to get herself out of this mess and back on the road to Los Angeles, and everything would look rosy again. Her parents, her brothers, her sisters and every other resident of Glenover, Iowa, might be satisfied living as faceless human beings in nowhere jobs, but she'd never be content with that. She was going to make her mark in this world.

No matter what she had to do.

MICHAEL WOLFE LAY IN BED, staring through the darkness, trying to keep his anger in check. He'd been called a lot of things in his life by people with vocabularies that could blow a freight train off its tracks, but *rapist* and *murderer* hadn't been among them.

He'd saved her, and this was what he got?

If only he'd realized how soon the storm was going to hit, he never would have set out for that bar tonight in search of Feliz Mendoza, a burglar on bail who'd decided to skip his court appearance. He never would have gotten caught in plunging temperatures and a sleet storm. And he never would have happened upon a half-frozen woman looking beyond pathetic, her dark hair plastered against her head, her sweater wet and misshapen, shivering so hard she could barely speak.

Given the fact that it was nearing midnight, sleet was pounding the city, the police station was four miles away and the women's shelter even farther, he'd brought her here. Then she'd shocked him by trying to run right back out into the same crappy situation he'd just rescued her from. Thirty more minutes on that freezing, deserted street without a coat could have put her in the hospital or worse, especially since there wasn't much of her to begin with.

But it wasn't until he'd hauled her away from the door, wrapped his arms around her and pulled her against him, that he realized just how small and delicate she really was. Suddenly he'd felt as if he was holding something terribly fragile, and if he made one wrong move, he'd break her. She'd felt all soft and willowy and…

He started to say *warm,* but she hadn't been warm in the least. She'd been a walking, talking, *screaming* ice cube.

Look at you! You're big, you're scary looking, and I'm pretty sure you could bite the head right off somebody's shoulders if you wanted to. What was I supposed to think?

Well, he had to admit that was nothing new. He'd been frightening people to death since he was thirteen years old, and now, at age thirty-one, the fear factor had only escalated. He was used to the world looking at him as if he ate little children and climbed tall buildings to swat at airplanes. And women certainly weren't exempt from that assessment. They all stopped dead in their tracks at the sight of him, and not because he was so damned good-looking. About the only women who didn't cross to the other side of the road when they saw him coming were those who were as tough as he was, who knew the streets, who'd seen far worse things in their lives than a man with a face like his.

So why had this woman's reaction bothered him so much?

Because she should have been thanking him for rescuing her instead of flattening herself against that door, breathing like a teenager in a horror flick and staring at him as if he was some kind of monster. *That* was why.

He didn't need this. He didn't need a crazy, argumenta-

tive, thankless woman bugging the hell out of him, disturbing the peace and solitude he valued so much. He'd never
brought a woman here and just the thought of her asleep in
the other room right now unnerved him. This was his space,
and he didn't share it with anyone.

Come tomorrow morning, he intended to remedy the situation. The quicker he got her out of here and she became
somebody else's problem, the better he was going to like it.

3

WENDY WOKE the next morning to sunlight shining brightly through a row of metal casement windows. Rising on one elbow, she looked around, and for a moment she wasn't sure where she was. Then she glanced down at the huge flannel shirt she wore and it all came back to her.

She slid out from beneath the covers and scurried to where she'd tossed her clothes over the chair last night. They were still cold and damp. Glancing at a clock in the kitchen, she saw it was nearly eleven o'clock. Had she really slept that long?

Then she sensed a much more pressing problem.

She'd once gotten caught in a New York cab in a snarl of traffic for over two and a half hours, but even then she hadn't had to pee as badly as she did right now. She adjusted the extra-extra-large shirt he'd given her until the neckline rested on her shoulders instead of halfway down her left arm and went in search of a bathroom. A minute later she reached a startling conclusion.

There wasn't one.

No. That was impossible. She circled the loft a time or two more, and suddenly it dawned on her that the bathroom could be only one place.

Inside his bedroom.

She walked to the door and tentatively pushed it open. Scanning the room, she saw a row of shelves along one wall overflowing with books and magazines. A lone dresser was positioned along another wall, and on top of it sat a portable television. Against the far wall was a bed, where he lay sleeping, stretched out on his stomach with the covers kicked off.

And he was stark naked.

She froze, stunned at the sight. *Back away. Leave the room. Pretend you saw nothing.*

But she couldn't. Not when her eyes were glued to the most beautiful male body she'd ever seen, and she'd seen her share. He had a physique as if he'd dropped right down from Mount Olympus, with gorgeous broad shoulders, just enough muscle to be hugely impressive without looking as if he'd popped a case of steroids and an absolutely world-class ass.

She'd known he was big. Rock solid. But she hadn't known just how flawless a body he had. It was like staring at a national monument or a hundred-story skyscraper or something else so awe inspiring that the only reason she'd pry her eyes away would be to haul out a camera. And stretched out beside him was the feline from hell, his one-eared head resting on the edge of the pillow, sound asleep. It was such a bizarre sight—the massive man and the gargantuan cat sleeping peacefully side by side.

But no matter how stunning the sight, she still had to pee. Badly. On the other side of the room, she saw the door leading to the bathroom. She tiptoed in that direction, but halfway there she heard the rustle of sheets and blankets.

The man had begun to move.

She stopped and flattened herself against the wall. He started to roll over, dislodging the cat. She thought about running from the room, but then he caught sight of her and she knew it was too late. As he turned and sat up on the edge of the bed, for a split second she was sure she was going to get a glimpse of the part of his body that would undoubtedly make the rest of him pale in comparison. But at the last moment he pulled the sheet along with him and rose from the bed, dragging it along as he walked toward her.

"What are you doing in here?"

She opened her mouth, but nothing came out. Her speech had deserted her completely. And no wonder. Every drop of her blood had rushed to the most demanding part of her body right now—her eyes. And at the moment they were roving over the exposed parts of his body as if they had a mind of their own, finally landing dead center on the part below his waist that he barely had covered up.

"Hey!" he said. "You want to look someplace else?"

Her gaze shot up to meet his. He spit out a breath of disgust and walked toward the bathroom. "Pervert."

Her eyebrows flew up. Pervert? He was calling her a *pervert*?

"Exhibitionist," she muttered.

He whipped around. "I live here! If you don't like it, you know where the door is!"

"Actually," she said, her attention playing over his body again, "I like it just fine."

She met his eyes again, and she swore that the big bad bounty hunter actually blushed. He turned and stormed toward the bathroom, slamming the door behind him.

Wow. Just...*wow*. She'd never in her life seen a body like that on a man, and the shock of it almost made her forget just how badly she had to pee. Almost.

She waited with extreme impatience and not a little bit of pain, and after a few minutes, she heard a flush. Thank God. It wouldn't be long now.

Then she heard the shower. *No, no, no!*

Ten long, agonizing minutes passed as she waited for him to come out, the mountain lion on his bed giving her the evil eye the whole time. Finally the man emerged, a towel wrapped around him this time, and his dark, wet hair slicked back. But instead of moving aside to let her in, he slowly ran both hands up either side of the door frame, blocking the entrance, nonchalantly flexing those awesome biceps and chest muscles.

"Going somewhere?" he asked.

She stared up at him. "Uh...the bathroom?"

"Oh, yeah?"

"Yeah."

Silence.

She shifted uncomfortably. "Do you think you could let me by?"

"Uh-huh."

"Like...sometime soon?"

"Uh-huh."

"When?"

"As soon as you get naked."

"Get *what*?"

For the span of several seconds, he just stared at her, a calculating expression on his face. Then she knew.

This was payback.

She rolled her eyes with disgust. "Look, I'm sorry, okay? How was I supposed to know you sleep naked?"

"You came into my room without knocking."

"I didn't want to wake you."

"I like my privacy."

"You can't be serious about this."

"Do I look like I'm joking?"

She eyed him carefully. "Truthfully? No. Actually, so far I haven't found you to be a particularly funny guy."

He eyed her up and down. "Off with it, sweetheart."

She huffed with disgust. "I am *not* taking off my shirt!"

"My shirt."

"Whatever."

Still he refused to move. She put her hands on her hips. "Just what do you intend to do? Stand there all day?"

"Nope. Not all day. But I can spare at least a few hours."

"Oh, just forget it!" she said, glaring at him. "I don't need your damned bathroom!"

"Suit yourself. But there's not another one within a mile of here. Not one you'd want to use, anyway."

"Well, I suppose that's what bushes are for, aren't they?"

"Good luck finding one. This isn't exactly the garden district."

He had her there. *Damn it.* How dare he keep her from one of the fundamental necessities of life for such a petty revenge?

Unfortunately, he could be as petty as he wanted to be because it would take a bulldozer to move him away from that door. How was she going to get out of this?

Okay. Maybe it really wasn't such a big deal. After all, during that cheap vacation in Mexico two years ago, she'd sunbathed topless on the beach. And there was the tiniest little possibility that she might have gotten caught on a *Girls Gone Wild* video flashing her boobs during a moment of Mardi Gras insanity. If he'd happened along during one of those times, he'd have gotten an eyeful, along with every other man in the vicinity. Was this really any different than that?

But there was a problem. One glance at her nearly non-existent breasts, and he was going to know he'd gotten the short end of the deal. He'd showed her the body of Adonis, and all she had to offer was Olive Oyl. Still, a man was a man, and there was a strong possibility that getting naked in front of this one would be like dangling raw meat in front of a lion.

All at once he put his palm against the wall beside her left ear and leaned in closer. She froze for several tense seconds.

His sharp, challenging expression, his rugged features and his intense, dark eyes made him look almost...sexy. In spite of the situation, she felt an odd stirring deep inside her, and she couldn't stop her breath from coming faster and her body from heating up. Then he slowly reached up and touched his fingertip to the top button of her shirt, and she was absolutely certain that she was going to end up naked whether she'd agreed to get that way or not.

"I told you I like my privacy," he said, his voice a malicious drawl. "And I meant it. So if I catch you sneaking in here again, it's all coming off. And I won't be responsible for what happens next."

To her immense relief, he stepped back, wearing that pissed-off expression that made him look like a prison guard on death row. She brushed past him, went inside the bathroom and closed the door behind her. She turned and leaned against it, sucking in a huge breath of relief and letting it out slowly, shocked as hell to still be clothed.

Then, out of nowhere, images sprang to mind of just what he might have meant by *I won't be responsible for what happens next*, and it occurred to her that taking that particular punishment might not be a totally negative thing.

Stop it. He's big, he's mean and he's threatening. A man you don't want to mess with.

She did her business, then decided that if he could avail himself of the shower, so could she. She found soap in there, some heavy-duty manly deodorant stuff with little green flecks of Irish whatever in it, but what the hell. Clean was clean. And the generic shampoo would hardly make her hair brittle if she used it just once. On the other hand, the hot water was heaven. For the first time since she'd been driving in her car last night, her body felt warm all the way to her bones.

Of course, there was still that pocket of cold desperation clinging to the inside of her stomach.

Right now, the man in the other room was the only ally she had within seven hundred miles, and she was pretty darned sure he didn't want her around any longer than necessary. But there had to be a way to persuade him to help her. She figured a trip to the police station to file a crime report would be a good first step. He'd at least take her there, wouldn't he?

Past that, she had no idea what she was going to do.

As soon as the woman slipped past him into the bathroom, Wolfe got dressed, then went into the kitchen and found her damp clothes hanging over the chair. He threw them into the dryer on the landing of the back stairwell, then sat down on the sofa and picked up the Metro section of yesterday's *Dallas Morning News*. A quick scan of the headlines told him he didn't really give a damn about any of it, and he tossed the paper to the coffee table again.

How was he supposed to concentrate on the newspaper when there was a naked woman in his bathroom?

He folded his arms, closed his eyes and listened to the shower running, imagining what her body looked like beneath that spray of water. *Damn.* He would have loved to have made good on his threat, to take a look at that sweet little body he'd had his hands on last night. In the end, though, he never would have done it, no matter how bold she seemed to be about wandering into his bedroom whenever she felt like it. He hated that feeling of somebody invading his space, disturbing his peace and quiet, and by the time this day was over, he'd make sure she was gone and everything was back the way it was supposed to be.

He heard the shower stop, and a few minutes later she emerged from his bedroom wearing his shirt again and a towel wrapped around her hair. She glanced toward the kitchen chair.

"Where are my clothes?"

"I put them in the dryer."

She smiled. "Well. That was nice of you. Thank you."

"You can't put them on wet. And you can't leave until you put them on."

Her smile evaporated, replaced by a look of resignation. She folded her arms across her chest and walked toward him.

"Look. I think we got off on the wrong foot here. I made you mad last night after everything you did for me, and then I came into your bedroom this morning and made you angry all over again. I'm sorry about that."

He just stared at her.

She eased closer. "You're supposed to say, 'Why, thank you, Wendy. I accept your apology.'" She paused. "That's my name. Wendy Jamison. And yours is...?"

"Wolfe."

Her eyes widened. "Is that a nickname?"

"Last name."

"And your first name?"

"None of your business."

She gave him a look of muted disgust, and he couldn't have cared less. It had been a long time since he'd felt the need to be on a first-name basis with anyone, and this woman was no exception.

"Just as soon as your clothes are dry," he told her, "I'll take you to the police station."

She let out a breath. "Thank you. I'd appreciate that."

She reached up and unwrapped the towel. Then she bent forward at the waist, wiggled her head and stood back up again, slinging her long, dark hair over her shoulders. She tilted her head and finger-combed it, letting it fall in damp, shiny threads down her back. The neck of his shirt had fallen aside, displaying her upper chest and left shoulder. Her skin was pale, more a product of genetics than the season. It was soft, smooth and unblemished—the kind of skin that looked as if it would bruise if he so much as whispered against it.

"Do you think the police will be able to recover my car?" she asked him.

"Nope."

Her face fell. "You're not much of an optimist."

"I'm a realist. I'm betting your car has already been chopped, packed and shipped."

She heaved a sigh. "To tell you the truth, that's what I figured. Unfortunately, everything I own was in that car and trailer. Including my five thousand dollars."

"Five thousand dollars?"

"Yes. In my glove compartment."

"What in the hell were you doing keeping that kind of money in your glove compartment?"

"I stopped by the bank as I was leaving New York. I wanted to get traveler's checks, but their computer was down, and I got tired of waiting. It was almost closing time, and I wanted to get on the road. So I told them to give me the money in cash."

"Bad move."

"Yeah," she said, "I know. Don't you just love hindsight?"

She sat down on the opposite end of the sofa, one leg curled beneath her, then leaned forward and rubbed her fingers up and down her other leg from her thigh to her calf, drawing his attention toward yet another expanse of her bare skin. Her legs were long, lean and delicate, and he wondered how they were even strong enough to hold up the rest of her.

She looked up at him. "Got any lotion?"

He glanced away. "Fresh out."

"Your razor was a little dull. Hard on the old legs."

Actually her legs weren't old at all, and they looked just fine to him. More than fine. And what in the hell was she doing using his razor?

"Bet you're wondering why I was heading to L.A.," she said.

The thought hadn't crossed his mind, but before he could respond, she answered her own question.

"I'm going to be an actress."

She said it with a bright little sparkle in her eyes, and he resisted the urge to roll his. A beautiful young woman heading to Hollywood to become an actress? There had to be a bigger cliché somewhere on the planet, but he couldn't imagine what it was.

"I know what you're thinking," she said, holding up her palm. "But trust me. I'm not some dumb little ingenue who's going to end up on a casting couch before she knows what hit her. I know what I'm doing." She turned on the sofa until she faced him, resting her elbow along the back of it. "See, I spent a few years trying to break in on Broadway, but the trouble there is that they want you to be talented. I am, of course, but there's a fine line, you know? Between pretty good and great? I don't think I'll ever cross that. I'm very self-aware. I know my limitations."

"So you think you can make it in Hollywood instead."

She made a scoffing noise. "Of course I can. Ever seen *Baywatch*?"

Good point.

"And I'm not going it alone. I've got an agent. He's a friend of a friend who has my head shots and résumé and thinks he can do something for me. Open a few doors. That's all I need, you know. A few doors opened so I can wedge my foot in.'' She smiled. ''And the rest, as they say, will be history.''

He knew she was impulsive, careless and argumentative. Now he could add *delusional* to the list.

''The trouble is,'' she said with a dejected sigh, ''I kind of lost everything I own last night. That leaves me in a pretty precarious position.''

She turned those big brown eyes up to stare at him plaintively, and Wolfe felt a twinge of sympathy. He had to admit that while he'd met lots of people down on their luck, she was a little further down than most.

No. She wasn't his problem. Pure chance was all that had led him to pick her up in the first place. He'd already done his good deed by letting her sleep on his sofa last night, and that was as far as he intended to extend his charitable contribution to the Society of Struggling Actresses.

''Do you have a family?'' he asked her.

''Of course. But they live in Iowa.''

''So call them.''

''I can't.''

''Why not?''

''I have eight brothers and sisters. My parents work at the local factory and barely make ends meet. They're lucky to put food on the table. The day I left town, I knew I'd be on my own. I promised myself I'd never ask my family for anything.''

''They wouldn't help you?''

''Yes. They would. They'd give me everything I need and go without themselves, because that's just what they do. So that's not an option.''

''Friends?''

''No point in going to that well. It's dry. I'm the rich one of the bunch.'' She settled back on the sofa, a pensive expression on her face. ''I can handle this situation. I just have to think, you know? Formulate a plan. I've been at rock bottom before and managed to climb out." She pondered the situation for a few moments more. "The first thing I need is a little walking-around money. A couple hundred bucks, just so I won't be destitute. Then I can start looking for a way to get to L.A." She raised her eyebrows questioningly. "Any idea where I could earn a little quick cash?"

Wolfe started to say no. Then a thought occurred to him.

He'd scoped out Mendoza at Sharky's last night, hitting a dead end because he couldn't get the guy alone long enough to grab him. If Wolfe walked into that bar, he was liable to be recognized, and Mendoza's buddies just might cause more trouble than Wolfe wanted to deal with. But if he could get her to lure Mendoza outside by himself, he could have him in handcuffs and into his car before Mendoza knew what hit him. After she did the job for him, he could give her some cash for her trouble, drop her off at a women's shelter, and his conscience would be clear.

"What are you willing to do for it?" he asked her.

"What do you have in mind?"

"There's a job I need to have done. I could go down to Harry Hines and pick up a hooker, but you'll do."

She narrowed her eyes. "Hey, I'm not sleeping with you, so get that out of your mind right now."

"It never entered my mind."

Well, that was a lie. But his random thoughts of the past half hour had nothing to do with the matter at hand.

"How much does the job pay?" she asked.

"You don't want to know what you have to do first?"

"Does it involve getting naked?"

"No."

"Then I'll do it."

"A hundred bucks. Of course, the wardrobe is coming out of your paycheck."

"Wardrobe?"

"I'll take you by the Trinity River Thrift Store. Cheap and trashy."

"So what's the job?"

"I'm going fishing."

"Yeah?"

Wolfe gave her a deadpan stare. "And you're the worm on the hook."

4

A FEW MINUTES LATER, Wolfe had given Wendy the gist of his plan, and she felt a tremor of excitement at the very thought of it. A hooker. He wanted her to play a hooker.

Hot *damn*. Character roles were so much fun.

Wolfe went to the kitchen, grabbed a box from a cabinet, then brought it back and dumped its contents onto the coffee table.

"What's that?" she asked.

"Breakfast."

She picked up one of the bars. "Protein Power?"

"Eighteen vitamins and minerals. Lots of fiber."

"Any room for flavor in there?"

"No pain, no gain."

She unwrapped one and bit into it. It tasted like sawdust and sand pebbles held together with Elmer's glue. In the time it took her to gag one down, Wolfe had eaten three. She'd barely disposed of her wrapper in the trash when he grabbed her clothes from the dryer, tossed them to her and told her to get ready.

After she dressed, Wendy asked Wolfe if she could make a long-distance call, promising to pay him for it out of the hundred dollars she was going to earn. She mentally ticked off her siblings in her head, finally deciding to call her oldest sister, Terri. Terri was levelheaded and nonreactionary and would tend to ask fewer questions than anyone else in her family. Good thing, since Wendy intended to fudge a little on the truth of her situation.

When Terri came on the line, Wendy told her that since she'd gotten sidetracked in Dallas because of the storm, she'd decided to stay there with a friend for a few days. True to Terri's nature, she didn't question a thing. She merely made Wendy promise to call her as soon as she left for Los Angeles again.

Wendy hung up the phone, glad she'd bought some time. Now all she had to do was formulate a plan to get to the West Coast that didn't involve taking money from her family.

Minutes later Wendy was following Wolfe down that big, creaky elevator to the first floor of the warehouse, where she was relieved to discover that the motorcycle wasn't the only vehicle he owned. First in line was a nondescript white van. Next to it sat a gleaming late-model SUV, which she'd have salivated over if she hadn't seen the black Porsche hiding on the other side of it.

"Oh, *wow*," Wendy gushed, running her hand over its fender. "Now, *this* is a gorgeous car."

"Hands off. We're taking the Chevy."

"Chevy?"

Wendy had been so preoccupied with the sports car that she hadn't noticed vehicle number four. Like a mangy mutt sidled up next to a purebred, an ancient Chevy Malibu sat next to the Porsche, its crunched left rear fender crisscrossed with rust and its yellow paint faded almost to white.

Wendy blinked with confusion. "You have a Porsche, and you're driving *that*?"

"We're going into a bad area. We have to fit the profile of the neighborhood."

"So when do you drive the other cars?"

"The van's for surveillance, and the others depend on what I'm doing or who I'm after."

Wendy looked longingly at the Porsche as she slid into the passenger seat of the Chevy. They left the warehouse and headed toward the police station. An hour later Wendy had filed the obligatory theft report with a very bored looking detective who had a splatter of coffee on his tie and a comb-over that hid nothing but his self-respect. It was pretty clear all around that she stood a better chance of getting hit by a meteor at midnight than recovering her car and belongings. It was a sickening feeling knowing she had literally nothing in the world but the clothes on her back, but she refused to give in to it. Instead, she let excitement take over.

After all, she was getting to play a hooker.

They left the police station. A few minutes later, Wolfe pulled into the parking lot of the Trinity River Thrift Store. He parked the Malibu in a space near the front door, giving Wendy a nice view of the establishment's dirty sign, dirty windows and dirty neighbors, squashed as it was between an adult video store and a condom shop.

They went inside. The place smelled like a hundred-year-old attic. Shelves were filled with various garage-sale items—lamps, glassware, dishes, bookshelves. Lining the back of the store were minor to major appliances that were not-so-gently used, along with a genuine antique walnut-veneer bedroom suite complete with missing hardware and beer bottle rings. And the clothes. It looked as if every woman in every sleazy trailer park in Texas had cleaned out her closets and donated them to an even bigger charity than herself.

The clerk, a twenty-something woman dressed in a pair of jeans and a too-tight sweater, came out of the back room. She had naturally frizzy but unnaturally blond hair and had clearly been the victim of a recent cosmetics counter explosion.

The woman took one look at Wolfe and stopped short, her mascara-laden eyes slowly widening as her gaze panned upward. Then she glanced at the cash register, as if she was expecting him to haul out a gun and demand all her money. Wendy didn't blame her. Her first look at Wolfe had been equally overwhelming.

"She needs clothes," Wolfe told the clerk, nodding toward Wendy. "Something flashy and trashy. You got anything like that?"

The clerk swallowed hard, as if trying to dislodge a boulder from her throat. Finally she pointed to a rack a few feet behind them that was filled with sparkles and spangles. Wolfe strode over, flipped through the clothes and pulled out an animal-print micro-miniskirt. Wendy took it from him, staring at it in disbelief.

"Sorry," she said. "I can't wear this. Synthetic leopards are an endangered species."

"You're playing a streetwalker, not a high-dollar call girl."

She held it up, twisting it one direction, then another. "I don't think this will even cover my rear end."

"Exactly."

Wolfe grabbed a minuscule black top with gold sparkles and handed it to her. She stretched it a couple of times. "Well, this'll fit my left pinkie. What else do you have?"

"Just put it on. What size shoes do you wear?"

"Five."

He dug through a nearby bin, tossing shoes left and right before coming up with a pair of monstrous black platforms. If this job included surveillance through third-story windows, she was going to be all set.

The clerk pointed her toward a short hallway leading to a

dressing room, where Wendy wiggled out of her jeans and into the skirt. Then she tossed her shirt and bra aside and pulled the stretchy top over her head and into place. She turned, looked into the mirror and froze.

Yes, the skirt was short. The shirt was tight. The shoes were stratospheric. But the clothes had caused a definite transformation toward the indecent.

This was *so* cool.

Dressing for a performance was always such an upper. It made her feel the character. *Be* the character. She blinked lazily into the mirror, then drooped her eyelids in a come-hither stare, visions of hot, mindless, well-compensated sex flowing through her mind. She ran her hands up her hips to her waist, then threw her arms back over her head and tousled her hair into a sexy mess, feeling a buzz of exhilaration at the sight of Wendy the Good Girl morphing into a hot, sexy lady of the evening. Wolfe was right. When in Rome, you had to dress like Roman hookers, or whatever that saying was.

But then she realized that part of the equation was missing, something no self-respecting prostitute would ever go without. She stuck her head out of the curtained dressing room and motioned to the clerk. The woman came down the hall.

"Got any makeup I can borrow?" Wendy asked.

"Uh...sure. Just a minute."

Wendy wasn't too keen on wearing another woman's makeup, but then she wasn't too thrilled about wearing another woman's clothes, either. Unfortunately, she was stuck with both.

The clerk returned with a cosmetics bag the size of a kangaroo pouch. Wendy thanked her and hefted it into the dressing room. A few minutes later, she'd put the *painted* in *painted lady.* After a final look in the mirror, she swept the curtain aside. With a pout on her lips and a swivel in her hips, she headed back down the short hall.

Stopping at the doorway that led into the main part of the store, she slid her hand slowly up the door frame and cocked her hip, planting her other hand against it. Wolfe turned and caught sight of her. He looked down her body to her legs and back up again, a slow, lingering appraisal that told her she'd definitely gotten his attention. *Yes.* She could feel it. She was every man's dream in one gold-spangled, animal-spotted, high-heeled package, and he couldn't take his eyes off her.

Then he zeroed in on her breasts. His usual frown deepened into an even more pronounced one, and he shook his head with disapproval. Her elation fizzled like a lit match hitting a puddle of water.

She dropped her hands to her sides. "What?"

Wolfe strode over to a table piled with various undergarments. He grabbed a bra and lobbed it to her. She stared down at it, unable to recall the last time she'd seen so much lace and Lycra all in one place. Anna Nicole Smith would have had trouble filling up this one.

He turned to the clerk. "Got a box of tissue?"

"Uh...no," she said. "No tissue."

"Toilet paper?"

She nodded obediently and scurried to the bathroom, as if Godzilla himself had threatened to eat Tokyo if she didn't hurry. She returned a moment later with a roll of pink toilet paper and handed it to him. He tossed it to Wendy. She stared down at the half-empty roll.

"You're kidding, right?"

"Do I look like I'm kidding?"

She searched his deadpan expression, looking for a little sparkle in his eyes, a little turn-up of his mouth. No such luck. The stone-faced presidents on Mount Rushmore were more likely to crack a smile.

She went back to the dressing room and put on the bra, trying to ignore the fact that it was a preworn garment, then started stuffing. Then she stuffed some more. It took most of the roll to fill up the cups, and when she finished she pulled the stretchy top down over them. She turned left and right, checking out her new profile in the mirror.

Boobs. She had boobs.

Hmm. So this was what it felt like.

She walked out of the dressing room. Wolfe stood waiting, his sharp focus zeroing in on her newly augmented bustline. She gave him a big smile and thrust her chest out for his inspection.

"So whatcha think? This is about as big as I can go before I'm a walking fire-code violation."

He turned away. "It'll do."

Yeah, he was trying to play it down, but still she could see it in his eyes. Like all men, it was pretty clear that Wolfe deemed excessive cleavage to be a major improvement, like adding a family room onto a tiny house. More recreational possibilities.

As they headed for the cash register, Wendy suddenly realized that with this skimpy outfit, the moment she stepped outside she was going to have goose bumps on her goose bumps.

"Hey, wait a minute," she said. "I'm not wearing much in the way of clothes here. It's cold outside."

"So buy a coat."

"A coat?" the clerk said, suddenly coming to life. "Oh! I've got the perfect one to go with that outfit! Wait till you see this!"

She trotted down an aisle and returned with a waist-length garment that looked like a patchwork of purple raccoon pelts. And the raccoon had clearly had a disfiguring skin condition.

"Isn't it just the *cutest thing?*" she gushed. "I was gonna grab it myself, but it's eight bucks, and I don't get paid till Friday. Besides, it'd look better on you with your hair color and complexion and all."

Wendy decided to take that as a compliment. But eight bucks? Right now, that sounded like eight thousand. Not that it wasn't a steal for such a stunning garment, but her hundred dollars was slowly dwindling away.

She turned to Wolfe. "You're paying for the coat."

"Excuse me?"

"It's up to you to provide me with adequate working conditions. Warmth is a basic necessity."

"But you get to keep it when you're through."

"Well, I should hope so. I didn't think you'd want to add it to your wardrobe."

He leaned in close to her and whispered, "But I might use it as a drop cloth to change the oil in my cars."

"Which would only make it more attractive," she whispered back.

He glared at her a moment more, then heaved a sigh of disgust. "Fine. I'll buy you the damned coat."

Wendy turned to the clerk. "I'll just wear this stuff out of here. Could I have a sack for my other clothes?"

"I'm out up here, so I'll get some from the back."

Wendy took the coat off the hanger, slid into it and checked out her reflection in a nearby mirror. "Ooh!" she cooed, looking back over her shoulder at Wolfe. "She's right! It's really *me*, isn't it?"

"Yeah," he muttered. "It's you, all right."

She gave him a sigh of mock disgust. "What's a girl gotta do to get a compliment out of you, anyway?"

"This is a job, not a date."

"Then I'm betting you have a lot more jobs than dates."

"My personal life is none of your business."

"Have you ever thought about smiling once in a while? Just a tiny bit?"

"Waste of energy."

"So you're always this crabby?"

He pulled out a twenty and tossed it on the counter, pointedly ignoring her.

"Having a bad day?"

He said nothing.

"Bad month?"

Not a word.

"Well, it certainly can't be a systemic problem. Not with those fiber-loaded power bars you eat. A few of those once a week and you'll never, *ever* have to worry about—"

He clamped his hand onto her arm and pulled her aside, dropping his voice to an angry whisper. "Do you want this job, or don't you?"

She blinked with surprise. "Of course I do."

"It requires shutting the hell up when it's necessary. And it's necessary from here on out. Do you think you can handle that?"

She raised her eyebrows. "So I'm supposed to play the sexy, *silent* type?"

"That's right."

She gave him a sly smile. "What if the guy wants me to talk dirty?"

Wolfe just stared at her, shaking his head slowly. The clerk returned. He grabbed the sack from her hand, stuffed Wendy's clothes inside and hustled her out of the store.

5

As Wolfe drove toward Sharky's, he felt more than a little unnerved by the woman sitting beside him. Not that she didn't look the part he wanted her to play. The clothes and makeup were right on the money, showcasing her body in a way that would make just about any man sit up and take notice. But he hated questionable outcomes, and he sensed one right now. Everything about this woman felt edgy and out of control.

Then again, all she had to do was get the guy to walk out the door of that bar. That was all. Any woman should be able to pull that off, especially one with a body like hers. Forget her unnaturally amplified breasts. Her legs alone would have Mendoza panting in her wake.

Wolfe brought his Chevy to a halt at a red light, then reached for his clipboard in the back seat. He flipped through the pages, grabbed a photo and handed it to Wendy.

"This is the guy. He jumped bail on a burglary charge."

Wendy took the photo. "Are you sure he'll be at the bar this early?"

"My informant told me that he's coming back today around noon for a game of pool. Grudge match. High stakes. He'll be there."

"So why don't the cops just pick him up?"

"Too many bail jumpers, not enough time. That's where I

come in. Once a guy misses his court date, the bondsman can send somebody after him. I'm that somebody."

"So if this guy is wanted by the police, why is he hanging out in a public place?"

"It's what guys like him always do. They'll change addresses, they'll change jobs, but they'll rarely change their routines. I've picked up guys everywhere from bowling alleys to pizza parlors to whorehouses. Anything they've done in the past few years, they'll continue to do."

"That's kinda stupid, isn't it?"

"Most criminals are."

"Why don't you just go in there and grab him? You've got to be bigger than this guy. I mean, like, *way* bigger."

"Because that bar is friendly territory for him, enemy territory for me. I've found a lot of guys in this area. If I show my face inside, somebody might recognize me, and all hell is liable to break loose."

"Do you really think anyone is going to mess with you?"

"Drunk lowlife? Yep. In a heartbeat. That's chaos. I don't like chaos. I like nice, calm apprehensions where nobody gets mad, nobody gets hurt, and nobody even realizes what's going on except the guy who's getting apprehended."

Wendy smiled. "Gee, that sounds kinda boring."

"Why? Because nobody's hauling out weapons and firing at anything that moves? Fine, then. It's boring. And I live to work another day."

"But what if somebody does pull a gun? You're not even armed."

"Don't bet on that."

She looked at his heavy coat, sweatshirt, jeans, boots. "I give up. Where's the weapon?"

"None of your business."

"Just wondering how lively this job is likely to get."

"Listen to me," he said. "I'm always armed. Always. But in thirteen years I've never once fired a weapon and I've never been fired on. Do you know why that is?"

"Why?"

"Because I don't take chances. And you're not going to, either. You're going to go into that bar, tell him you'll take him to heaven for a hundred bucks, and get him out the door."

Her eyebrows shot up with surprise. "A hundred bucks? Is that all I'm worth?"

Wolfe couldn't resist. "I don't know. Is it?"

She leaned closer to him, her face easing into a smoldering expression, her voice becoming a deep, throaty purr. "No way, baby. I'm *priceless*."

She continued to stare at him, her dark brown eyes so hot and provocative that he felt a shot of pure lust. In the span of a few seconds, he saw himself ripping that tiny little skirt right off her, then digging through that hideous pile of toilet tissue to get to the really nice stuff underneath. And then—

Then he heard a horn honk.

He looked over his shoulder to find the driver behind him pointing. He spun back around to see that the light had turned green.

Wendy settled back in her seat with a satisfied smile. "Ha! Gotcha, didn't I?"

Wolfe blinked with surprise, then finally woke up. He hit the gas a little too hard, and the Chevy lurched forward. "What are you talking about?"

"Can I play the part, or what?"

What was he supposed to say to that? The truth? Which was *Hell, yes?*

"Don't get cocky. This guy isn't completely stupid. He'll smell a setup a mile away."

"Don't worry," Wendy said, dropping the sun visor to

check out her lipstick in the mirror. "He'll never know I'm not one-hundred-percent lady of the evening."

Wolfe pulled into the parking lot of the liquor store next to Sharky's. He reached into the back seat again and grabbed some communication equipment from a box resting on the floorboard.

"What's that?" Wendy asked.

"A wireless receiver. Put it in your ear. No one will be able to see it. That way I can talk to you the whole time."

Wendy took it and stuck it in her ear, fiddling with it until she was satisfied. "Okay. It's in."

Wolfe pulled out a transmitter about half the size of a fountain pen and handed it to her. "This will allow you to talk to me, and for me to listen to what's happening. Stick it into your bra and leave it there."

For the first time, Wendy's brows drew together with concern. "Exactly how dangerous is this situation, anyway?"

"As long as you're wired and I'm listening, there's nothing to worry about. I can be in there in a matter of seconds if something goes wrong."

Wendy nodded.

"But there's no reason for anything to go wrong. Just get him out the door, and I can have him in cuffs and into the back of the car before he knows what hit him."

"Oh, I'll get him out the door. Believe me."

"Now, listen to me," Wolfe warned. "I'm running this show. Even if everything looks okay to you, if I tell you to get out of there, you get out of there. Immediately. No questions."

Wendy nodded. "But if that happens, do I still get paid?"

"As long as you do exactly what I tell you to do, you'll get the hundred bucks. Got that?"

"Roger."

"Okay. Get out of the car and make your way over there.

Once you're inside, I'll pull up as close to the door as I can and wait for you to come out."

"I can do this," she told him, a note of excitement in her voice. "I really can. I'm a good actress. Just watch me." She patted him on the arm. "One bail jumper coming up."

She got out of the car and headed for the bar, walking like the self-confident streetwalker she was supposed to be, and Wolfe's gaze was glued to every move she made. But as hot as she looked with that dark hair cascading over her shoulders and that little rear end shifting back and forth inside that microscopic skirt, it wasn't the glitz that got his attention. It was knowing what was under the glitz. In his mind's eye, he saw her standing in his living room this morning wearing nothing but his shirt, her dark hair wet and glossy and her face shiny clean without a speck of makeup in sight. Man, oh *man*, what a pretty picture that had been.

A guy like Mendoza, though, would be zeroing in on the flashy surface stuff, and Wolfe wondered if maybe he'd gone too short with the skirt and too tight with the shirt. Every man in that place was going to be lusting after her, and for some reason that thought sent the strangest feeling of protectiveness sweeping through him.

He brushed the sensation aside, only to have it come back even stronger when she strode past the alley that ran between the liquor store and the bar. Two men hovered in its shadows, eyeing her as she walked by. Wolfe sat up straight, prepared to jump out of his car and right into their faces if they so much as leaned in her direction.

"Wendy," he said into the microphone, "don't slow down. Just keep on walking past those guys."

"They're looking at me," she whispered back. "They think I'm a hooker. I can tell. That's good, right?"

"Hell, no! Don't start advertising until you get inside!"

He heard her sigh. "Yes, boss."

She toned it down a little, glancing away as she passed the men. Fortunately, they contented themselves with looking but not touching, so Wolfe's plan wasn't over before it even got started. He waited until Wendy slipped inside the door, then started the Chevy and crept it into the parking lot of the bar, hoping to hell he wasn't going to regret this.

SHARKY'S TURNED OUT to be just as grubby on the inside as it was on the outside—a dark, loud, ugly little bar filled with pool tables and questionable-looking patrons, all of them looking like criminals, and enough smoke in the air to knock another hole in the ozone layer.

She spotted Mendoza right off the bat. He was playing pool at a table in the corner beneath a glowing neon beer sign. Short and squat, he practically needed a stepladder to take a shot.

Wolfe's voice crackled in her ear. "Wendy? What's up?"

"Mendoza's here," she said. "Playing pool. I think he just finished a game."

She watched as he appeared to collect some money from the man he'd been playing with. As he pocketed the bills, a big-haired blonde sidled up next to him. She wore a fuzzy red sweater with a neckline that fell halfway to China and shiny leather pants so tight they had to be cutting off the blood supply to her legs. She leaned in and said something to him. He nodded, then turned and headed toward the bar.

Wendy felt a surge of excitement. The curtain was going up.

As Mendoza slid onto a bar stool, she made her way around the bar to the empty seat beside him and sat down, crossing her legs and turning toward him invitingly.

"Well," she said. "Looks like this is your lucky day."

He eyed her up and down at the same time he grabbed a

pack of cigarettes out of his pocket. "Oh, yeah? And why is that?"

She smiled invitingly. "You won your pool game."

He lit the cigarette and dragged deeply. "Luck had nothing to do with it."

"Well, then maybe you're feeling generous, huh? Buy a girl a drink?"

She let her coat fall open a little and thrust out her phony breasts. Mendoza's eyes fell right onto them, which was no problem at all. His eyes could fall from outer space and there would still be plenty of toilet paper in her bra to cushion their landing.

"Sure, baby." He pried his eyes away and nodded to the bartender. Wendy asked for a gin and tonic.

"You must be a really good pool player," she told Mendoza. "That's impressive."

He shrugged nonchalantly. A moment later, the bartender brought Wendy's drink. She sipped it, feeling the heat of the gin slither all the way down her throat.

"How long have you been playing pool?" Wendy asked.

"Since I was a kid."

"Ah. So that's why you're so good."

Wolfe's voice snapped in Wendy's ear. "Cut the small talk and get to the point. You're not trying to get him to take you to the prom."

Wendy ran her fingertip down Mendoza's arm. "So what do you say we finish these drinks, then take the party somewhere else?"

Mendoza's brows cocked up with interest. "That's a possibility. Depending on how much the party is going to cost me."

But before Wendy could respond, the woman who'd been talking to Mendoza earlier slid onto the bar stool on the other side of him. She flicked an angry look toward Wendy, then touched Mendoza's shoulder.

"Now, I thought you were going to get us drinks," she said. "Did you get lost on the way back?"

Mendoza gave the woman a big smile. "Course not, baby. Just taking a rest for a minute." He nodded to the bartender and told him to bring the woman a drink, and it suddenly dawned on Wendy that, judging from the woman's mode of dress and manner of speaking, they'd just put Mendoza in the middle of a hooker sandwich.

"Wendy?" Wolfe said. "What's going on?"

"I think I've got competition," she whispered back. She turned her head and played with her hair so Mendoza wouldn't hear her. "And damn it, she's *blond*."

"So get his attention again."

Wendy leaned in and traced her fingernail down Mendoza's arm. "Hey, baby. I was just about to tell you what I've got on the menu for today. Surely you want to hear about that, don't you?"

Before Mendoza could open his mouth, the other woman glared at Wendy. "Beat it, twinkie. I was here first."

Wendy drew back indignantly. "*Excuse* me?"

The woman got up, stalked over to Wendy, grabbed her off her bar stool and pulled her aside, whispering hotly, "I've been playing that guy for the past half hour, waiting for him to win that pool game and pocket that wad of cash! He's mine!"

Wendy folded her arms. "Well. I'd say that's up to him to decide."

"He's already made his decision!"

"Oh, yeah? If that were true, you'd be out the door by now, wouldn't you?"

"Wendy!" Wolfe whispered. "Don't get in a fight with

that woman! Back off! You do *not* want to mix it up with her!''

Oh, she didn't? Why didn't she? Wendy didn't remember a time in her life when she'd backed down from a challenge, and she'd be damned if this two-bit hooker was going to break her record.

"Is it my fault you can't hang on to your customers?" Wendy said.

"Ever hear of professional courtesy?"

"Ever hear that all's fair in love and war?"

"Oh, yeah?" the woman said. "So it's *war* you want? I'll give you *war!*"

Mendoza stabbed out his cigarette and slid off his seat, looking back and forth between them with the dumb but delighted expression of a man who was rarely the subject of one woman's interest, let alone two. "Now, ladies, there's really nothing to fight about here. What say we make it a threesome? That way, everybody's happy."

"Oh, good *God!*" Wolfe muttered in Wendy's ear. "That's it, Wendy. Get out of there!"

No. She wasn't going anywhere. She had a job to do. She was a good actress, and she could out-hook this hooker any day of the week.

She eased toward Mendoza. "We don't really need her, do we? Believe me—with what I've got in store for you, another body would only get in the way."

"Forget her," the other woman told Mendoza. "With me, you'll think you've got *three* women in the room. And you'll only be paying for one."

Mendoza's eyes widened appreciatively. Then he glanced at Wendy. She hadn't counted on a sexual tennis match, but the ball was in her court, and she had every intention of whacking it right back over the net. Thinking fast, she described a sexual interlude she'd heard about once involving a shower, a bar of soap and a position only a contortionist could hope to maintain. As soon as the words were out of her mouth, Wolfe's voice exploded in her ear.

"Wendy! Will you shut *up?* I told you to get out of there!"

But Wolfe couldn't see Mendoza's eyes lighting up like a kid at Christmas. As long as she had the upper hand, what was the point of throwing in the towel?

Unfortunately, the other woman dismissed Wendy with a wave of her hand, then described a sex act that didn't even sound anatomically possible. But by the expression of interest on Mendoza's face, he seemed quite willing to find out if it was.

"Sure," Wendy said, bringing her fists up to rest on her hips. "That sounds really great. But will she do it for sixty bucks?"

The other woman's eyebrows shot up. "Sixty bucks? Are you kidding? I've got bills to pay!"

"Wendy!" Wolfe said. "She's liable to start swinging. *Get out of there!*"

The woman's lips tightened with anger. She turned to Mendoza. "How about fifty?"

"Forty," Wendy said.

"Thirty," the woman countered.

Mendoza grinned, then turned to Wendy. "Your turn, baby. Do I hear twenty?"

She raised her chin defiantly, deciding it was time to sink her competition once and for all. "I'll do it for nothing."

Wolfe groaned in her ear. "Wendy! Don't tell him that! He's going to suspect—"

"That's right," Wendy went on. "Today is free sample day. No charge. What do you say to *that?*"

"No!" Wolfe said. "You can't give it away! He's going to know something's up! *Get out of there right now!*"

But Wolfe clearly didn't recognize the power of the word

free, especially when related to sex. A big grin spread over Mendoza's face.

"Free sample? Well, I can't hardly turn that down, can I?" He turned to the other woman. "Sorry, baby. If you can't beat free, we've got nothing else to talk about."

"You're damned right we don't." She turned to Wendy with a scoffing noise. "Sister, you are *nuts.*"

As she flounced away from the bar, Wendy felt a rush of elation. Why hadn't she thought of this in the first place? Didn't everyone on the planet want something for nothing? *Ha!* That cheap little hussy wasn't quite cheap enough, was she?

"Hey, guys!" Mendoza called out to a couple of his buddies. "This one's giving it away for free!"

"Free?" one of the men said. "Is she crazy?"

"Probably," Mendoza said. "But why do we care?"

We? Wendy froze. Uh-oh.

It didn't take long for the situation to catch the attention of two other men who likewise appeared to be attracted to the word *free.*

Big uh-oh. What was she supposed to say now? Would they believe her if she told them they had to have a coupon?

"Wendy!" Wolfe shouted in her ear. "Get out here now!"

"Can't," she whispered furtively. "They're all around me."

"Hey, Mendoza," one of the men said, "there's no need to go out in the cold. Benny's got that room upstairs."

What?

Mendoza tossed down the last of his drink and smacked the glass down on the bar. "Sounds good to me."

"Wolfe!" Wendy whispered. "They want me to go upstairs. What do I do?"

"Hang on, sweetheart," he said. "I'm on my way."

Mendoza took Wendy by the arm and led her across the

6

WOLFE SPED ALONG Industrial Boulevard, gripping the steering wheel so tightly his fingers turned white. It was too damned bad he had only one set of handcuffs, because he would have taken great joy in snapping a pair on Wendy, too. And maybe leg shackles for good measure. Or just a good old-fashioned straitjacket.

No. Forget that stuff. Tape. That was what he needed. A nice big piece of duct tape to slap over that mouth of hers, which hadn't been able to stop moving.

A long silence stretched between them, broken only by the hum of the heater and the hiss of the steam blowing out of Wolfe's ears.

Wendy tapped her fingertips on her knee. "So. I guess you're a little pissed off at me, huh?"

"Pissed off?" Wolfe said. "You think I'm pissed off? You haven't even *begun* to see me pissed off!"

"Now, Wolfe—"

"I told you to get out of that bar. You didn't do it. We both nearly ended up getting our heads blown off!"

"But it's the outcome that's important, isn't it?" She nodded over her shoulder to Mendoza in the back seat. "One more bail jumper bites the dust."

Wolfe smacked his foot down on the brake, wheeled the Chevy into a convenience-store parking lot and slammed it into Park. He turned to Wendy, his voice tight with anger.

"I hate gunfire. Did I tell you how much I hate gunfire?"

"But you carry a gun!"

"That doesn't mean I like it when somebody pulls a trigger!"

"I don't know why you're so angry. Everything turned out okay."

"You caused chaos. I hate chaos. A beautiful woman offering free sex to a barful of drunk men? I've seen recipes for disaster, sweetheart, but that tops them all!"

She smiled. "So you really think I'm a beautiful woman?"

Wolfe looked at her incredulously, on the verge of pounding his head against the steering wheel. Her digression was an amazing thing.

"What I really think," he told her, "is that you're lucky you didn't end up having to give those guys what you promised them!"

She shrugged. "I wasn't worried."

"Then you were the only one who wasn't!"

"No. Seriously. I knew nothing was going to happen to me."

"Oh, yeah? And how could you have been so sure of that?"

"Because you told me so. You said as long as I was wired and you were listening, I wasn't going to get hurt. I believed you. And you were right."

She peered at him, those brown eyes wide, clearly going for the helpless doe-eyed look. Unfortunately, it was working. Not once in his life had he ever considered himself a sucker for anything, but those eyes...

Damn.

"I'm sorry," she said with a sigh. "I really am. You're right. You were the boss. You told me to do something, and I didn't do it."

He exhaled. "Wendy—"

"No. You have a right to be angry. So if you need to yell some more, it's okay. Really. Go ahead. Yell. I deserve it."

He slumped with disgust. What was he supposed to do now? If she told him to yell, it took all the juice out of it. He just sat there, gritting his teeth so tightly his jaw ached.

"Thank you for saving me," she said. "That's twice in two days. I guess that kind of makes you my hero, doesn't it?"

Wolfe blinked with disbelief. Hero?

No. That was a crock. A great big crock of manipulation designed to keep him from being mad at her, and he wasn't buying it. He reserved the right to be angry about this from now until the turn of the next century.

How had this happened? How could he be berating her one minute, only to have her turn everything around until she was a damsel in distress and he was a knight in shining armor? She was overlooking the fact that she was a damsel who'd gotten *herself* in distress, and this particular knight should be banishing her to the dungeon forever.

She blinked those big brown eyes again. "So are you still mad at me?"

"Yes!"

She smiled. "No, you're not. I can tell. Your voice is angry, but your face isn't."

He shot her a narrow-eyed glare.

"Nope. It's still not. That's a trying to look mad face, not a really mad face."

"Well, isn't that just the sweetest thing?" Mendoza said from the back seat. "So are you two gonna kiss and make up?"

"Shut up," Wolfe muttered.

Then Mendoza started making little kissy noises, and it was all Wolfe could do not to reach over the seat and make sure he never used those lips again. Wolfe's job depended on him commanding respect, but with Wendy yapping about him being her hero and all that other nonsense, he couldn't have commanded respect from a teenage shoplifter. Ever since he'd picked Wendy up off the street last night, his clean, orderly existence had been turned upside down, and he couldn't deal with it any longer.

Big brown eyes or not, before this day was out, she was history.

WOLFE DROVE to the county jail and transferred Mendoza to the officers there, all without uttering another word. Wendy guessed that he'd barked all he was going to about the issue and now he was just going to fume in silence.

"Where are we going now?" she asked him.

"Bail bondsman."

Ah. To collect his money. Which meant she'd collect her money. A very good thing.

"After you get paid," Wendy said, "do you think you can give me my hundred dollars in cash? Minus whatever the clothes cost, of course."

"What makes you think I'm paying you anything?"

Wendy felt a shot of panic. "What are you talking about?"

"You didn't follow instructions," Wolfe said sharply. "I told you to lure him *out*, not lure me *in*. If I'd wanted to grab him by stomping in there and kicking ass, I'd have done it already. You didn't do the job, so you don't get the money."

Wendy opened her mouth to speak, then shut it again. As much as she hated to admit it, he was right. Now that she thought about it, Wolfe had come into that bar only because she'd gotten herself into trouble, and now she expected him to pay her because he had the privilege of rescuing her?

She looked down at her clothes. "What about these? If I didn't earn the hundred, I can't pay you for them."

"I already have plenty of drop cloths. They're all yours."

Oh, how nice. She always scrambled at the last minute for a Halloween costume, and now she had one for years to come.

A few minutes later, Wolfe pulled into the parking lot of Lone Star Bail Bonds, which was nothing but an old double-wide trailer with a little rust here and there and gravel spread out front to resemble a parking lot. He killed the Chevy's engine.

Wendy tried to quell the flutter of anxiety she felt in her stomach. She'd been counting on the hundred dollars so she'd at least have the feeling that she wasn't totally desti-tute. But what was she going to do now?

Then she saw the sign in the office window. She froze, staring at it with disbelief.

Did it really say Help Wanted?

She felt that familiar little twinge she always did when-ever an opportunity presented itself that seemed to be just a smidgen beyond pure chance. Her wheels began to spin, telling her that if she could earn enough money to live here for a short while, she could buy another car and a few other necessities, then get back on the road to L.A. Once there, she could get a job to earn the rest of her money.

"Stay put," Wolfe said, opening the driver's door.

Nope. She had a job interview to go to. "I need to go to the bathroom."

Wolfe sighed. "Come in, then. But make it quick."

Inside the building, a woman in her mid-thirties sat be-hind a desk, a telephone pressed to her ear. Only one word could describe everything about her.

Plain.

Plain brown hair, plain brown eyes, plain beige shirt and

slacks, and as she spoke on the phone, a plain number two pencil flew across the pages of a plain yellow notepad.

She hung up the phone, still scribbling. "Hey, Wolfe," she said without looking up.

"Hey, Ramona." He tossed the bail ticket down on her desk. "Got Mendoza."

"Good. I hate that guy. Maybe this time they'll throw away the key."

"I've got a line on Rudy Pagliani. I should have him by tomorrow."

"That would also make my day." For the first time Ramona looked up, zeroing in on Wendy, wearing the tight, watchful expression of a woman who didn't take crap from anyone. "Who are you?"

"Your new..." Uh-oh. She didn't even know what job she was applying for. "Employee."

Ramona looked at Wolfe. "Is she with you?"

"At the moment."

"What's she talking about?"

"I don't know," Wolfe said, staring at Wendy. "What *are* you talking about?"

"I'm applying for the job. The one on the sign in the window."

"I thought you were going to California," Wolfe said.

"I can't go anywhere until I have some money in my pocket." She turned back to Ramona. "Tell me about the job."

"Clerical stuff. Answering phones. Filing. Correspondence."

"I can do those things."

Ramona eyed Wendy up and down. "Sorry. I'm looking for someone a little more...dressed."

"No! You don't understand. I don't usually wear these kinds of clothes!"

"So you're a hooker looking for a day job."

"No. I'm an actress looking for a day job." Wendy sat down in the chair beside Ramona's desk. "See, I was passing through downtown Dallas last night on my way to Los Angeles when I was carjacked. He got everything I own. I was standing out on the street all alone in the sleet without a coat and freezing to death, and Wolfe saw me and rescued me. Then today he dressed me up like a hooker and let me do a job for him. I was supposed to lure Mendoza out of a bar—"

"Which she screwed up," Wolfe said.

"Which is beside the point," Wendy said sharply, looking back at Wolfe, "since I'm not applying for a job at a whorehouse."

Ramona leaned back in her chair, rubbing her nose with a tissue. "Do you have any experience?"

"No. Not really." She paused. "Well, I once played the role of a secretary in an off-Broadway production. Actually, it was so off-Broadway that it was practically in Jersey, but still."

"So you're not really a secretary. You just play one on the stage."

Wendy brightened. "Exactly."

Ramona reached for another tissue. "This isn't a job where a pretty face gets you by. You're going to be dealing with good people, bad people and everyone in between."

"I'm very adaptable."

Ramona blew her nose. "Are you married?"

"No."

"Got any kids?"

"No."

"Are you pregnant?"

Wendy drew back. "Is it legal to ask that stuff in a job interview?"

"Nope."

"No. I'm not pregnant."

"Do you smoke?"

"No."

"Use drugs?"

"No."

"Have an ex-husband, boyfriend or Internet stalker with a temper, who tends to follow you to work with a gun in each hand?"

Wendy smiled. "I'm guessing you've had some employee problems in the past."

"You don't know the half of it."

"What does the job pay?"

Ramona named a figure that wasn't the most money Wendy had ever made in her life, but it certainly wasn't the least.

"Works for me," Wendy said. "Now, I am eventually going to California, so I might not be able to work for very long."

"Whatever. Can you start tomorrow?"

"You bet."

"You're hired."

Wolfe looked at Ramona incredulously. "You're hiring her? Just like that?"

"Hey, I've run an ad in the *Morning News* for the past week. Exactly two people have applied for the job—a woman with six kids who wanted to bring four of them to work with her, and a man who wanted to work inside a metal building so aliens couldn't read his mind. Hell, *yes,* I'm hiring her."

Wendy held out her hand. "I'm Wendy Jamison."

"Ramona Stockard," the woman said, then drew back as if she was going to sneeze. She fumbled in the tissue box, only to find it empty. Wendy reached into her bra, pulled free a wad of toilet paper and held it out. Ramona stared at it strangely, but grabbed it. A moment later she let loose with a sneeze that rocked the walls.

Wendy grinned. "See how handy I am to have around?"

Ramona sniffed miserably and dabbed her nose. "You always stuff your bra?"

"Only when I play a hooker. My secretarial boobs aren't nearly this impressive." She looked down at herself. "Speaking of which, I'm a little uneven now. I'd better go unstuff myself."

She started to trot off, only to turn back with a questioning look. "What did you say my job title is again?"

"Peon," Ramona said.

Wendy smiled. "Well, I shouldn't have any trouble living up to that, should I?"

As she headed off to the bathroom, Wolfe just shook his head. He'd never seen anyone who could talk themselves into and out of situations the way that woman could.

"So, Wolfe," Ramona said with a sly expression. "I've never seen this side of you before."

"What side is that?"

"The side that picks up sweet young things off the street and dresses them like tramps."

Wolfe felt a headache coming on. No, actually, it was just an extension of the same headache he'd had ever since the moment he'd first laid eyes on Wendy.

"I can't believe you hired her," he told Ramona. "That woman is a loose cannon."

Ramona shrugged. "She seems pretty sharp to me."

"I didn't say she was stupid. I said she was unpredictable."

Ramona sat back in her chair. "So maybe I'm a sucker for a hard-luck story. It appears you were, too, when you picked her up last night."

"What was I supposed to do? Let her stay out on the street and freeze? She slept on my sofa last night. That was all."

"Hmm. So where's she sleeping tonight?"

"At a women's shelter."

Ramona sat up straight. "You're taking her to a women's shelter?"

"What else am I supposed to do with her?"

She gave him a look of utter confusion. "Are you blind? Fate dumps a cute little thing like her right in your lap, and you don't know what to do with her?"

"Get your mind out of the gutter, Ramona."

"For once, I wish you'd get your mind *into* the gutter."

"My personal life is none of your business."

"Oh, will you cut that out? Our personal lives have always been each other's business."

She was right. Few people on this earth knew anything about him at all, and Ramona was one of them. Which meant that she had to know just how much a woman like Wendy would drive him crazy. Yet Ramona was still looking at him as if he was the one who was a few cards short of a full deck.

Ramona stared at him long and hard. "For once in your life, would you get a life?"

"I've got a life."

"You know what I mean." She nodded down the hall. "Why not start with her?"

Wolfe made a scoffing noise. "She's already driven me half nuts. I'm not interested in taking the rest of the trip."

"Maybe you need a little insanity in your life. And a little something else, too. Know what I mean?"

"Oh, yeah. I know what you mean. And if the day ever comes when I need somebody to analyze my sex life, you'll be the first person I call."

Ramona sighed. "You're hopeless, you know that?"

"No more hopeless than you are. When's the last time you got laid?"

"I've got a business to run. And the boys don't exactly hang around my locker waiting to ask me out." She blew her nose again. "Oh, hell. Face it, Wolfe. We're both hopeless."

Ramona wrote him a check for the apprehension, which he was sticking in his wallet just as Wendy came out of the bathroom. The cavernous bra and the twenty pounds of toilet paper that had been stuffed inside it were gone, and now that stretchy little top was left to cling to the real thing. Most men's attraction automatically leaned toward bigger than smaller, but Wolfe would take perfection over size any day. It appeared the old adage was true—the best things really did come in small packages.

"Let's go," he told her, pretending that he hadn't been staring.

"Uh...where exactly are we going?"

Those big brown eyes again, this time looking very wary. Suddenly he felt like crap for what he was about to do, but did he really have a choice? Did he want this woman underfoot any longer, turning his life upside down?

"I'm taking you to a shelter."

Her face fell. "No. Please don't make me go to one of those places. Let me stay with you a little longer."

"No way. I told you I like my privacy."

"Just for a few weeks until I get on my feet again."

"I said no."

"I'll clean your apartment."

"It's not dirty."

"Do your laundry."

"No, thanks."

"Wash your cars?"

"Nobody touches my cars."

"Even the Chevy?"

"I put dirt *on* the Chevy."

"Oh, come on, Wolfe! Isn't there something I can do for you in exchange for sleeping on your sofa a few nights?"

"Try food," Ramona said. "He doesn't eat worth a damn."

"No kidding," Wendy said. "You should have seen what we had for breakfast this morning."

"Those god-awful power-bar things?"

"Yeah. I've never tasted anything so disgusting in my life. If you had a million or two of them, you could build a bunker that even a nuclear bomb couldn't—"

"Hey!" Wolfe shouted. "You two want to shut up?"

Wendy smiled. "Now, is that any way to talk to your new live-in gourmet cook?"

He stared at her with utter disbelief. *No* was a very short word. What part of it did she not understand?

"My cooking is legendary," she went on. "Wait until you taste my chicken teriyaki."

"Not interested."

"Duck à l'orange?"

"Nope."

"Lobster Newburg?"

"No way."

His stomach was used to plain and simple food. All that orange Newburg teriyaki stuff would only clog his blood vessels and send his cholesterol through the roof, and he wasn't about to give in to something like that.

No matter how good a home-cooked meal sounded.

"Wait a minute," Wendy said. "I know the problem. You just don't want anything that swims or cackles." She put her finger against her chin, then gave him a calculated look. "How about beef Wellington?"

Red meat? Now, that was a little more like it.

"Beef Wellington," Wendy repeated, drawing out the words seductively. "New potatoes. Broccoli in garlic-butter sauce. French silk pie for dessert. And maybe a nice bottle of Australian merlot. How does that sound?"

Wolfe thought about the dozen or so TV dinners sitting in his freezer right now. Piles of pasta with a few scraps of chicken. Three of those almost made a meal.

Then he thought about beef Wellington.

Wendy stared up at him hopefully. Ramona *tap-tap-tapped* her pencil against her desk, giving him a look that said she reserved the right to berate him about this through eternity if he said no, and he sure as hell didn't want that. Just because Wendy cooked him one meal didn't mean he had to let her stay around forever, did it?

He twisted his mouth with disgust. "Okay. You can make dinner, then stay overnight."

"How about two weeks?"

Wolfe looked at her incredulously. "I said *one night!*"

She blinked helplessly, injecting a note of shameless pleading into her voice. "Ten days?"

He glared at her. "Through the weekend, and that's it."

"How about a week?"

He slumped with resignation. "You are *such* a pain in the ass."

Wendy smiled. "One week it is."

"*One night*," he said sharply. "Unless I decide otherwise."

"And just when will you be making this decision?"

"I don't know. It just might depend on how good a cook you really are."

"Well, then. I just might be staying for a very long time."

This was a mistake. Wolfe could feel it in his bones. But something about the way Wendy was looking at him, her face all bright and cheerful, gave him a few seconds of feel-good he hadn't expected. And then there was Ramona, that tiny smile on her lips that told him she was thinking something she wasn't saying, even though he knew exactly what that something was.

Get a life, Wolfe. And why don't you start with her?

7

WOLFE TOOK WENDY by the grocery store, where she loaded up on enough food to feed a third-world nation. After they brought the groceries to Wolfe's apartment, she shooed him out the door, telling him if he wanted a masterpiece he had to leave the master alone to create it. He started to tell her that he had no intention of being kicked out of his own apartment, only to realize that it was probably a good thing. He wasn't used to another person rattling around anywhere near him, so if he stayed, she'd only end up driving him even crazier than she already had.

But now, as he ascended the warehouse elevator two hours later, he felt a twinge of foreboding. After all, he'd left a crazy woman alone in his apartment playing with fire.

Don't worry. Everybody's good at something. She's a gourmet cook. She knows her way around a kitchen.

He shoved his worries aside, instead letting visions of the first decent dinner he'd had in months roll through his mind. Then the elevator doors opened, and he smelled it.

Smoke.

He rushed to the door, banged on it. "Wendy!"

Without waiting for her reply, he fumbled for his keys and unlocked the door, tearing it open just in time to see her yank a pan out of the oven. She tossed it onto the stove top with a clatter, then backed away, waving her arms to clear the smoke that was pouring off it.

"What the hell is going on?" Wolfe shouted.

She shot him a look of distress, still fanning. He approached the incinerated pile of meat, staring down at it with total disbelief.

She looked at him sheepishly. "I guess I burned it a little."

"A *little?* I've seen five-alarm fires without this much smoke! How did this happen?"

"Well, it was supposed to be cooked at three-hundred-and-fifty degrees, but I was short on time, so I thought if I set it at five hundred—"

"You don't cook anything at five hundred degrees!"

She opened her mouth to respond, but nothing came out. Wolfe inched closer, narrowing his eyes. "You lied to me."

"No," she said, holding up her palm. "Now, it wasn't a lie. Not exactly."

"You said you were a gourmet cook! You practically burned the building down! You don't call that a lie?"

"I just don't have my usual...you know. Utensils and stuff. Pots and pans and knives and measuring cups—"

"Are you kidding? You wouldn't know a Crock-Pot from a crock of—"

"Okay!" she said, throwing up her hands. "I lied! I'm not a gourmet cook! I'm not any kind of cook! I barely know how to order a pizza!"

He looked at her with utter disbelief. "Then what in the *hell* made you think you could cook something like this?"

She sighed. "While you were in the produce aisle, I sneaked a peek at a cookbook. I've got a good memory." She paused. "But I guess not good enough."

"You come from a family with nine kids! How did you miss learning how to cook?"

"I hated cooking, so I always swapped chores with my brothers and sisters. I made a lot of beds and cleaned a lot of toilets instead."

Wolfe looked around. "What about the rest of dinner?"

Wendy closed her eyes. "You don't want to know."

She was absolutely right. He didn't.

Wolfe flipped on the vent over the stove, which did very little to suck up the smoke, so his apartment was going to smell like an incinerator for a week. If he was smart, he'd hustle her down the elevator, into his car and out of here, and hope for the sake of the world at large she never rattled a pot and a pan again.

Wendy poked at the pile of charred beef. "Actually, you know, it might not be as bad as it looks."

"Oh, yeah? Tell me how it's not as bad as it looks."

"Well, the meat is burned, yes, but it can't be black all the way through, can it? And only the potatoes around the edge of the pan are crusty. And the pie—well, it might be all right if we use spoons and think pudding instead. Now, the broccoli's a goner, but even I can't screw up a bottle of wine." With a bright smile, she grabbed a knife and fork. "Here. I'll dig around in the meat a little and see how deep the black part goes."

She turned to her task, acting as if they were embarking on some kind of exciting adventure together.

"Look, Wendy..."

"Oh, good! Some brown stuff!"

"Wendy—"

"And even some pink. See?"

He sighed. "I just don't think this is going to work out."

She paused a moment, then started carving again, her voice a little shaky. "What do you mean?"

"I mean that I was right the first time. I don't think you should be staying here."

Her face fell, and she lay down the knife. "Oh."

"I think it would be best for both of us if I took you somewhere else."

For several seconds she just stood there, not moving. She

swallowed hard, then slowly turned her eyes up to meet his, and his heart skipped with apprehension. Those big brown eyes were one thing. Those big brown eyes swimming in tears were something else entirely. She pursed her lips, and a tear rolled down her cheek.

He fumbled around, grabbed a dish towel and held it out to her. "Come on," he said awkwardly. "Don't cry."

She nodded, but the tears kept coming.

"Maybe it's time for you to call your family and ask them for money," Wolfe said.

"I can't do that to them. They'd have to scrape too hard to help me." She dabbed at her eyes with the dish towel. "And I shouldn't be doing this to you, either. It's wrong for me to ask you to let me stay here when you've done so much for me already."

Wolfe sighed. "Look, I don't get it. Why is this such a big deal to you? I mean, look around you. This place isn't very nice. And neither am I most of the time. So why do you want to stay here?"

"Because I—" She shrugged weakly. "I—I guess because even though I act like all of this is no big deal, getting carjacked, losing everything I own, the truth is that I'm alone, and I'm scared, and—" she paused, her voice a plaintive whisper "—I feel safe with you."

Safe? With him?

Wolfe just stood there, dumbfounded. When she looked at him, she had to see the same hard-edged face, mammoth body and don't-screw-with-me expression every other woman on the planet saw. Yet every word out of her mouth, every move she made, said she didn't. In a world where he'd spent his entire life scaring people to death, she was telling him just the opposite.

In that moment, his anger went up in smoke right along with the smoldering chunk of beef. He couldn't do it. No matter how much grief she'd caused him, he knew there was no way he could drop her off at one of those places where she'd be just a face in the crowd, one more down-on-her-luck woman who nobody cared enough about to help so strangers had to do it. Okay, he was a stranger, too, but not as strange as those people would be, and...

Oh, *damn.*

She dabbed at her eyes some more, but the tears kept coming, and he had no idea what to do to make them stop.

He sighed. Yes, he did.

"Never mind," he said. "You can stay."

She rolled her eyes. "You're just saying that because I'm crying. As soon as I stop—"

"No. I mean it."

"Sure. You say that now, but—"

"You can stay."

"I know men hate a crying woman. They'll stand on their heads and sing show tunes if that's what it takes to get her to stop."

"I said you can stay. Does it really matter why?"

"I just want you to know that I'm not trying to manipulate you. I swear I'm not. I just cry a little too easily sometimes. I—I can't help it."

"Wendy—"

"And I've had a lot to cry over for the past day or so. Still, if that's the only reason you're letting me stay—"

"Wendy!"

She sniffed. "What?"

He leaned in and spoke slowly and distinctly. "If I were you, I'd quit while I was ahead."

In spite of the no-nonsense look he gave her, a tiny smile warmed her tear-streaked face. "So you're really not going to kick me out?"

"No. I'm not going to kick you out."

"So how long can I stay?"

"Hell, I don't know," he muttered. "For now. That's the best I can do. But you have to salvage something out of this dinner. I haven't gotten any less hungry in the past five minutes."

Her smiled widened. "Yeah. Okay. There's bound to be something edible in this mess somewhere, right?" She wiped her cheeks with the dish towel, her whole body heaving with relief, then picked up the knife and started in again on the charcoal beef briquette. As she sliced away, she began to hum. The noise should have driven him crazy, but instead it was a soothing sound, like a waterfall, or wind rustling through treetops.

He couldn't believe it. She was actually happy to be here.

No. Happy to be safe. Happy not to have to pay rent. Happy not to be on a cot at a women's shelter. That was a far cry from being happy to be here.

Or happy to be with him.

I feel safe with you.

Well, she'd feel safe with a bazooka on each shoulder, too. It had nothing to do with him, and everything to do with him living in a fortress. Or maybe in the end it just came down to the fact that she didn't like the idea of sharing a bathroom with forty other women.

In any case, he'd probably let her stay a week. Just until she got on her feet. Okay—maybe two weeks if that was what it took until she could get an apartment deposit together. Of course, if Ramona's pay period hadn't cycled around, it might be three weeks, but that was absolutely it. After that, she could cry buckets, and he wasn't going to be the least bit moved. He was going to hustle her right out the door, and there wouldn't be anything she could do to change his mind.

To HER OWN SURPRISE, Wendy managed to salvage enough of the food to make a decent dinner, then even got Wolfe to admit that while it wasn't the best meal he'd ever eaten, it certainly wasn't the worst. And the wine made everything seem as if it didn't matter all that much, anyway. Afterward, she sent Wolfe to the living room, insisting on tidying up the kitchen herself. Her cooking sucked, but cleaning she could handle, and after everything that had happened she figured it was the least she could do.

Wolfe sat down on the sofa, flipped on the TV to a cable news station, then opened up the newspaper. Out of nowhere, the cat from hell slithered over and leaped up beside him, curled himself into a ball and closed his eyes, his head resting against Wolfe's thigh. It all seemed so domestic that, for a moment, Wendy felt like June Cleaver, until she realized that June probably wouldn't have set foot in the sleazy side of downtown Dallas, Wolfe didn't resemble Ward in the least and any pet of the Beaver's would have had all of his appendages intact.

After she finished in the kitchen, she brought their glasses and the remainder of the bottle of wine into the living room, wanting to make this situation feel as normal as possible for both of them. She sat down on the sofa gently so as not to disturb the domestic tranquility of man and cat. But as soon as her fanny hit the cushion, the cat leaped up, tore off the sofa and sat six feet away, glaring at her with those wicked yellow eyes.

Wendy slumped with dismay. "Maybe I'm a little sensitive, but I don't think your cat likes me."

Wolfe never looked up from his newspaper. "He doesn't like anybody."

"He seems to like you just fine."

"He's just kissing up. He knows where his food comes from."

Nope. Dogs kissed up. Cats would starve before hanging out with a human they didn't like.

"Do you keep him inside all the time?" Wendy asked.

"Hell, yes. This is a bad neighborhood."

"Well, he looks like a pretty bad cat."

"Nope. He's a real wuss."

"Hard to believe."

"Oh, yeah? If he could kick another cat's ass, would he be missing half his body parts?"

Good point.

"So what's his name?"

He shot the cat a dirty look. "Weenie."

She laughed a little. "Weenie?"

"He ran into the warehouse one night to get away from a dog."

She looked at the cat, wondering why the floor hadn't collapsed under his weight. "Must have been a big dog."

"Oh, yeah. Had to weigh at least five pounds. Damned cat could have turned around and sat on the stupid thing and squashed him flat." He looked down at the cat and made a scoffing noise, then turned back to his newspaper. "He ran away like his tail was on fire."

"It was nice of you to take him in," Wendy said.

"I didn't have much of a choice."

"Sure you did. You could have left him out on that street, scared to death. But you didn't. I guess it's lucky for him that you're the kind of guy who picks up strays." She paused. "I guess it's lucky for me, too."

Wolfe glanced up at her, suddenly looking very uncomfortable. He folded his paper, then looked down at the sofa where he sat.

"Uh, listen...you probably want to go to sleep. I'll just—"

"No!" she said. "You don't always go to bed this early, do you?"

He paused. "No. Not usually. But I can go to my room and read, or something."

"No! We've still got wine to finish, don't we? Let's stay up and watch something on TV."

The last thing Wendy wanted to do was drive him out of his own living room at seven o'clock in the evening. That would make him uncomfortable. And the more uncomfortable he felt with her there, the more likely he was to want her to leave.

She grabbed the remote and began to flip through the stations, every hit on the channel button causing the television to spit out a loud static noise.

"Wendy—"

"Doesn't look as if there's much on tonight," she said, still flipping. "But I'll find something." She zoomed past a talk show. A decorating show. A game show.

"Oh, look! It's that new reality show! The one where three couples and a marriage counselor go into the Amazon with only the clothes on their backs, army rations and a—"

"Will you give me that?" Wolfe pulled the remote out of her hand. He checked his watch, then pushed a couple of buttons, taking him directly to what looked like one of those urban cop shows.

"There you go," Wolfe said, setting the remote down next to him. "Some quality programming."

"Sure," Wendy said, pouring them both a little more wine. "Why not? I haven't had my quota of extreme violence today."

"And from now on," Wolfe said, picking up his glass, "I'm in charge of the remote."

He said it with such authority that she almost laughed out loud. Like that was a big surprise? A man declaring himself chief-in-charge of an electronic device?

Wendy settled back on the sofa, tucked her legs up beside

her and leaned against a pillow. Wolfe sat with his feet propped up on the coffee table, his arms folded over his chest, watching the show with the same intensity with which he did everything else.

After a while, Weenie overcame some of his feline disgust at Wendy's presence on the sofa and leaped back up next to Wolfe, who began to stroke him absentmindedly. It was a strange and wonderful sight—a man powerful enough to tie a python into a pretzel petting that abysmal-looking animal.

Wendy kept stealing sidelong glances at Wolfe, and pretty soon she wasn't following the TV show at all. Her mind kept wandering back to how he'd kept her from freezing on the street last night, how he'd stomped into that bar to save her and how, even though she'd messed up so much, still he'd taken her in. Little warm fuzzies started coming to life inside her, and a feeling of security and well-being wrapped itself around her like a warm blanket.

Soon, though, security and well-being weren't the only feelings she had.

After half an hour, her eye muscles were worn out from looking at him without looking if she was looking, at the same time the attraction she felt toward him was growing exponentially. And her mind was exhausted from telling herself how crazy that was. Now that she was actually co-existing with her landlord without the two of them snapping at each other, the last thing she needed to do was to rock the boat with all these sexy thoughts.

Sexy?

That made no sense. He wasn't classically handsome by any means, with a ruggedness to his face that would have made a lumberjack look like an underwear model. And that scar on his cheek made him seem downright dangerous. So why was her heart suddenly going crazy just because she was in the same room with him?

It had to be his gorgeous body. What woman with two functioning eyes wouldn't be drawn to that?

No. That made no sense, either. She could go to a gym and watch buff bods right and left and not feel half as hot as she did right now.

It had to be the wine.

Well, she knew that was a lie, too. She'd once downed half a dozen tequila shots on a Florida beach, then danced until dawn. Two glasses of wine might make her a little woozy, but she was hardly one of those women who thought any man looked good after a couple of drinks. Alcohol just made her observations a little more focused.

And boy, were they focused right now.

When the first TV program was over, Wolfe turned to another one, and then another one after that. His attention remained on the television while Wendy's attention remained on him.

Finally ten o'clock came. Wolfe turned to her. "It's getting late."

Wendy couldn't help yawning. "Yeah."

He flipped off the television, then reached into his wallet, pulled out some bills and tossed them onto the table.

"What's that?" she asked.

"A hundred dollars."

She stared down at it with surprise. "But you said you weren't going to pay me."

"I'm not. It's just a loan. I expect it back. And I'm keeping track."

"Of course. I've got a job now. I can pay you back soon."

"Have you thought about how you're going to get there?"

"Huh?"

"To your job tomorrow morning."

Wendy stared at him. Unfortunately, that little problem hadn't yet crossed her mind. "Public transportation?"

"They tried that once down here. Somebody torched one of the buses."

"Oh. Then I suppose a cab's out of the question, too?"

Wolfe tossed a set of car keys onto the table beside the money. She gave him a questioning look. "You're letting me borrow your car?"

"I don't need it tomorrow."

"The Chevy?"

"Right."

"I don't suppose..."

"No, you can't drive my Porsche."

She smiled. "Can't blame a girl for trying."

He said something about getting her something to sleep in. Disappearing into his bedroom, he returned a moment later and handed her one of his shirts, along with a portable alarm clock. She caught a whiff of the same scent she'd smelled the night before.

"Mmm," she said, pulling the shirt to her nose. "Nice fabric softener."

He frowned. "I hate static cling."

The domestic image that created was so at odds with his image as a big, tough bounty hunter that it was all Wendy could do not to laugh. And what did a man like Wolfe need with fabric softener, anyway? She had no doubt he could hold up a shirt and scare the static electricity right out of it.

"Good night," he said, and started to walk away.

"Wolfe?"

He turned back. She took a few tentative steps toward him. "I screwed up a lot of things today. Thanks for letting me live."

"This is the state of Texas, sweetheart. Murder comes with a big price."

She smiled. "You saved my life, loaned me a hundred

dollars and you're letting me use your car. You've got too much invested in me to kill me now."

They stared at each other a moment more, and all at once Wendy felt those warm fuzzies multiplying inside her like bunnies on Viagra. She took a few steps forward, stood on her tiptoes, pressed her palm against one side of his face and kissed his opposite cheek.

"Thank you," she said. "I don't know what I'd do without you."

She meant it as an act of appreciation. A sincere gesture of thanks with nothing else attached. Not a single thought about anything more *personal* had crossed her mind.

At least, not until she stood so close to him that she could practically feel his heartbeat.

Suddenly all those hot, sexy thoughts she'd been having about him all evening coalesced into one gigantic rush of sexual awareness. The air between them seemed to grow hot and heavy, as if her steamy thoughts were oozing out of her mind and filling the scant space between them. She rocked slowly down to her heels, letting her hand fall from his cheek to his shoulder.

Then she looked up at him.

Oh, boy.

The moment she met his dark eyes, crazy little shivers sizzled between her shoulders. Only a few seconds passed, but it felt like a hundred. She touched her tongue to her lower lip, then took that same lip between her teeth. His eyes moved down to her mouth, hovered there for a moment, then rose again, a gesture that could mean only one thing. As impossible as it seemed, he was going to kiss her.

And she couldn't think of anything she wanted more.

She stared up at him, her lips actually tingling with anticipation, waiting...waiting...

"I have an early surveillance tomorrow," he said suddenly, backing away as he spoke. "So I have to leave before dawn. I'll try not to wake you."

All at once, the erotic possibilities she'd felt between them evaporated like drops of water on a summer sidewalk, and the delicious anticipation she'd felt turned to confusion.

Wait a minute. Where do you think you're going? Get back here and kiss me!

She swallowed hard, trying to find her voice. "Uh...don't worry about waking me. I can usually sleep through anything."

He simply nodded, then disappeared into his bedroom, closing the door behind him and leaving Wendy standing alone in the sudden silence, wondering what had happened to that imaginary warm blanket that had surrounded her all evening.

Answer: it had turned into a wet one.

She collapsed to the sofa with a sigh of frustration, hugging Wolfe's shirt, the scent of the fabric softener wafting up to her nose again and making her want him even more. Well, *damn.* She'd looked up at him with her best kiss-me expression, and he'd backed away as if she'd caught fire. Why?

After a few more minutes of feeling deprived and depressed, she forced herself to look at things logically. Why *shouldn't* he have backed away? After all, hadn't she caused him nothing but trouble since the moment she walked into his life?

It was time she faced facts. He was tolerating her. Nothing more. No matter how much he protested to the contrary, the only reason he was even letting her stay was because she'd cried. It was a guy thing. A man would do anything to get a woman to stop crying, including giving in and let a total stranger be his roommate for an undetermined period of time. Undoubtedly he was counting the days until she was finally out of his life. And while he was counting the days, she should have stuck to counting her lucky stars instead of insisting on having the moon, too. After all, he'd given her a roof over her head, a car to drive and money in her pocket. What more could she want?

Simple question, simple answer: a nice, slow, steamy kiss from the most intriguing man she'd met in a long time. *That* was what.

Give it up. Not gonna happen. How much clearer could he have made it?

With a heavy sigh, she told herself it was for the best. Things seemed to be fine between them now, and she needed a place to stay more than she needed to get up close and personal with a sexy man. Okay, so she had to work a little to make herself believe that, but soon the practical side of her brain won the argument. She told herself that from now on, no matter how many times she stared at him with fuzzies in her tummy and lust in her heart, she was going to keep her feelings to herself.

WOLFE WENT into his bedroom and closed the door behind him, his heart still beating in his chest like machine-gun fire, thinking that if he had to spend one more evening with Wendy like this one he was going to go crazy.

If his life depended on telling somebody about the shows they'd just watched, he'd be a dead man. All he'd been able to think about the whole time was the woman on the other end of his sofa, her legs curled up beside her, sipping wine and occasionally brushing a strand of that gorgeous dark hair away from her face. He thought he would hate having somebody invade his apartment, particularly a woman who drew gunfire, burned things and had one hell of a time monitoring her mouth.

He didn't hate it at all.

It had been ages since he'd had an eligible woman within speaking distance whom he wasn't hauling off to jail. Now he had one of the most beautiful women he'd ever seen in his living room and he didn't know what to do with her.

No. That wasn't true. Contrary to what Ramona thought, he knew quite well what to do with her. But he also knew that the minute he did it, she'd turn tail and run. And could he really blame her when he had a face that would scare a person out of ten years' growth?

He went into his bathroom, turned on the light and looked at himself in the mirror. Really looked. Nope, nothing had changed. He still had eyes that could make a prison-hardened criminal think twice about messing with him, along with that damned scar that made him look as if he'd come out on the losing end of a bar fight. Most of the time, his face served him well. His job depended on him looking like a badass, and he'd never done anything to diminish that image. It'd be bad for business.

Have you ever thought about smiling once in a while? she had asked him. *Just a tiny bit?*

He opened and closed his mouth, squinted his eyes, then tried to smile. It felt as if he was creaking open the hinges of a hundred-year-old crate. Finally he got his lips to turn up, but only his mouth was smiling. The rest of his face refused to get the message.

After a few more ridiculous-looking attempts at appearing cheerful, he gave up, telling himself that he was what he was, and there was nothing he could do to change it. Did it really matter, anyway? That little peck on the cheek had just been Wendy's way of saying thanks, and only a complete idiot would have taken it for anything else.

Still, the way she'd looked up at him...

In those few seconds, all he saw was that full mouth, those gorgeous lips and those beautiful brown eyes that seemed to be calling to him like a siren song, and he could have sworn...

No. It was wishful thinking. Nothing more. Kissing a man like him in a situation like this was, without a doubt, the very last thing on Wendy's mind.

8

AS SOON AS WENDY ARRIVED at Lone Star Bail Bonds the next morning, Ramona gave her a crash course in the bail bond business, then introduced her to the two men who worked for her. Lonnie was a stick figure of a man with an unlikely mop of salt-and-pepper hair and a perpetually lonesome expression, while Ralph was short and stout and looked as if he'd never met a buffet he didn't like. Both of them spent most of the time on the phone when they were in the office, then made periodic runs to the jail to secure the release of people who'd been arrested once everything was in order for their bonds to be posted.

Both men greeted Wendy with smiles, which was a real upper. She knew what it was like to have a job where she had to work with sourpusses, and she was thrilled that this wasn't going to be one of them.

After her condensed training session, Wendy answered her first phone call.

"Lone Star Bail Bonds," she said cheerfully.

On the other end of the phone was a woman whose teenage son had been arrested on drug charges. Wendy directed the call to Ralph, then looked up at Ramona.

"How was that?"

"Lose the perkiness. People call here because they're in trouble or they know somebody who is. The last thing they want to hear is Barney the Dinosaur on the other end of the line."

Wendy nodded, and the next time she answered the phone she put on her serious phone voice. It kind of made her sound like Joe Friday asking for *just the facts, ma'am,* but Ramona seemed pleased.

Okay. So far, so good.

About halfway through the morning, Ramona told Wendy she could take a coffee break, and Wendy asked if she could make a couple of quick long-distance calls. She phoned her sister Terri again and told her the whole truth about what had happened. When her sister flipped out a little, Wendy gave her Wolfe's number and her number at work, telling her not to worry, that she had a job and a place to stay. Terri would pass that information on to her parents, who would probably be calling to hear firsthand that she really was all right, but Wendy would deal with that when the time came. Then she called her agent in Hollywood to tell him what had happened and that she was going to be delayed indefinitely, letting him know how he could get in touch with her, too.

"So," Ramona said offhandedly, as Wendy hung up the phone. "Did you and Wolfe have a nice dinner last night?"

"Uh...yeah." Wendy winced. "Well, we might have, except for one tiny problem."

"What's that?"

"I can't cook."

Ramona blinked with surprise. "You mean all that gourmet cooking stuff was a lie?"

"Not exactly. I mean..." She sighed. "Well, okay. Yeah. Unfortunately, dinner turned out to be a little...lacking."

Ramona glanced out to the parking lot. "Looks like you drove Wolfe's Chevy here this morning."

"Yeah. That was nice of him, huh?"

"So even though dinner wasn't quite up to par, you're still staying with him?"

"Yeah."

"How long is he going to let you stay?"

Wendy sighed. "He didn't really say."

"But he didn't say when you had to go?"

"No. He didn't."

Ramona smiled a little, then glanced back down at the file she held. "Good. That's good."

Wendy had already figured out that Ramona was one of those people who never said all of the things she was thinking. She definitely had a lot of lines that needed reading between, but damned if Wendy could do it.

Around noon, using part of her lunch hour and some of the money Wolfe had given her, Wendy hopped into the Chevy and ran over to Trinity River Thrift Store. The clerk recognized her immediately and started to suggest a few items of clothing related to the lovely purple coat she was still wearing, but Wendy opted for normal stuff—jeans, shirts, sneakers. Then she stopped at an actual store and bought undergarments. If she washed everything tonight she'd have clothes to wear for the rest of the week. It was a real upper to be clothed again. That meant she was getting control of something in her life. *Yes.* Things were definitely looking up.

Ramona had offered to buy Wendy's lunch if she'd swing through a drive-through and pick up burgers for everyone, so she stopped at McDonald's on her way back from shopping. She'd just returned to the office, doled out the food and sat down at her desk to eat, when a man walked through the door.

He looked to be in his late twenties, wearing a pair of camouflage pants, black boots and a black turtleneck sweater. His sandy-blond hair was swept away from his face, and he had eyes so blue she could make out their color at ten paces. He stood at least six feet tall with a carefully sculpted body that said he never missed a workout. As he sauntered across the office, Wendy's first thought was that he was a pretty hot guy. Her second thought was that he thought so, too, which pretty much canceled out her first thought.

The man started toward Ramona's desk, then caught sight of Wendy. She could almost see a pair of antennae shoot right out the top of his head and, like a guided missile, he changed course and veered toward her desk.

"Well, look at this," he said, stopping to stare down at her. "The view has sure improved since the last time I was here."

That had to be some kind of record. In the span of fifteen seconds, he'd reduced her to an insignificant piece of eye candy.

"Ramona?" he said. "Aren't you going to introduce me?"

"This is Wendy Jamison. Wendy, this is Jeremy Slade. He's a bail-enforcement agent."

"Forget that politically correct crap," Slade told Wendy, folding his arms over his chest. "I'm a bounty hunter. That's right, baby. I hunt people for a living."

Wendy stared at him dumbly. Was this guy for real?

"So what are you doing for lunch?" he asked her.

He didn't appear to be blind, but somehow he'd missed the hamburger, fries and cola on her desk. "Well, I was kinda thinking maybe I'd eat this hamburger."

"Trash it. Let's go out."

"Sorry," Wendy said, dragging a fry through ketchup. "I'm a tightwad. Can't stand to let anything go to waste." She tossed the fry into her mouth.

"Then forget lunch. How about dinner tonight?"

Wendy shook her head, still chewing. "I have plans."

She did. TV dinners with Wolfe. Or if Wolfe wasn't going to be home, she'd eat with Weenie. In spite of his personality defects, he'd be far better company than the man standing in front of her right now.

"Tomorrow night, then," Slade said.

"Gee, I have plans then, too."

He sat down on the edge of her desk, dropping his voice dramatically. "I'm a bounty hunter, you know. A very dangerous man. How about it, Wendy? Do you like dangerous men?"

Wendy just sat there, dumbfounded. Was she the only woman on the planet who didn't buy this kind of crap? Then she glanced at Ramona in time to catch her rolling her eyes.

Nope. Not the only one.

Just then the door opened, and Wolfe walked into the office. Wendy sat up straighter, her heart skipping wildly. He met her eyes for a brief moment of acknowledgment, then sat in the chair beside Ramona's desk and got right down to business.

Something had definitely changed since last night, something Wendy had tried to dismiss as nothing more than a reaction to the fact that he'd taken her in and protected her and made her feel safe when her whole life had fallen apart. But if that were true, then why was she getting all flushed with excitement when all he'd done was walk through the door?

Even in the midst of that confusion, though, there was one thing of which she was absolutely certain. He had a body to die for, and if Pretty Boy didn't move his butt off the edge of her desk and quit blocking her view, she was going to deck him.

Then she glanced up at Slade and realized that she wasn't the only one whose attention was focused on Wolfe. He drew a deep breath that expanded his chest, then raised his chin a few millimeters and replaced his betcha-think-I'm-sexy expression with an irritated frown.

Hmm, Wendy thought. *Tension.*

She looked back at Wolfe, expecting him to meet Slade's taut reaction with one of his own. But he never even glanced in Slade's direction. He tossed a bail ticket down on Ramona's desk.

"Got Pagliani."

"Good," Ramona said. "I know he was a tough one."

"Oh, will you give me a break?" Slade called out. "My grandmother could have brought that guy in. If I hadn't been out of town, he'd have been behind bars a week ago."

Wendy's attention shot over to Wolfe, whom she fully expected to stride across the room, yank Slade up by his collar and do some serious rearrangement of his facial features. But for some reason she couldn't hope to fathom, Wolfe never even looked in Slade's direction.

To Wendy's surprise, Slade stood up and sauntered over to Ramona's desk. "Hear you brought Mendoza in, too," he said in a mocking tone. "Another highly dangerous apprehension."

Okay. For some reason, this man had a death wish. Why else would he be instigating a pissing contest with a man who could squash him like a bug? Slade was a big guy, but Wolfe was bigger. *Way* bigger. Still, even with his smart mouth, Slade could have been on Mars for all Wolfe was acknowledging him.

"I've got another one here," Ramona said a little sheepishly, "but you're not going to be happy about it."

Wolfe opened the file, and his face fell. "Rico? God, Ramona—"

"I know, I know," Ramona said, holding up her palm. "Don't rub it in."

"Didn't I tell you he had *run* written all over him? You never should have posted bond on that guy."

"Yeah," Ramona said, sighing. "But he had a nice mother with a pocketful of cash. She cried. You know how I can't stand it when they cry."

Wolfe sighed. "Okay. The cops will be looking for him hot and heavy. Whenever they find out where he's holed up, it'll probably take SWAT to pull him out." He handed her back the file. "Let's let it ride for a while. If we're closing in on ninety days and the cops still haven't pulled him in, I'll see what I can do."

"Oh, for God's sake," Slade muttered, pulling the file out of Ramona's hand and then glaring at Wolfe. "You know, for a guy who's supposed to be so damned tough you sure do wimp out on the hard stuff."

Wendy had never been a fan of bloodshed, and she was sure she was getting ready to witness some now. But Wolfe merely looked through a few more files with Ramona, taking one more and sticking it under his arm. Wendy was dumbfounded. Why wasn't Wolfe shutting the man's mouth once and for all?

Slade walked back over to Wendy's desk, leaned against it and opened the file he'd taken from Ramona. He extracted a mug shot and flashed it in front of Wendy. "There he is, baby. That's the face of a kidnapper. Scary, huh?"

The guy in the picture had a weak chin, approximately three hairs left on his head, and horn-rimmed glasses. He looked like a depressed IRS agent. The only reason she'd be scared of that face was if she'd cheated on her income taxes.

"Yeah," Slade said, "it's dangerous work, but I'm bringing him in. And as soon as Rico is behind bars again, why don't you and I go out and celebrate?"

For the first time since he'd walked through the door,

Wolfe turned slowly and stared at Slade, his eyes narrowing into slits, his jaw tightening ever so slightly.

"Wendy," he said.

She gave him a pleasant smile. "Yes, Wolfe?"

"Don't worry about dinner tonight. I'll pick up a pizza on the way home."

"Sounds good."

"Pepperoni okay?"

"Perfect."

Wolfe picked up the files Ramona had given him and headed for the door. He gave Lonnie and Ralph a nod, then left the office, the door clicking shut behind him.

Slade stared after him, his jaw practically dragging the ground. He turned to Wendy. "So *he's* your plans tonight? Wolfe? You're dating *him*?"

"No. Not exactly."

"Well, thank God."

"I'm living with him."

Slade's expression was so flabbergasted that Wendy almost laughed out loud.

"You're kidding," he said.

"Kidding? Why would you think that?"

"Oh, come on!" Slade laughed a little. "A woman like you? A man like him? Where in nature does that happen?" He shook his head. "Sorry. That just doesn't add up."

She smiled sweetly. "Then maybe you need to change the battery in your calculator."

Slade gave her a frozen look of surprise, as if he had to wait a moment for *that* to compute. Then he stuck the mug shot back into the file and slapped it shut. "Tell you what, baby. As soon as you get tired of sitting in King Kong's palm, let me know. I'll show you a *really* good time."

Slade had a few more words with Ramona, then sauntered out the door.

"Damn it," Ralph muttered, smacking his fist against the desk. "I thought for *sure* today was the day!"

"Nope," Lonnie said. "Not gonna happen."

"But Wendy's here, so the little bastard had somebody to show off for. And then Wolfe showed up, Rico was up for grabs..." Ralph sighed. "All the ingredients were there."

Lonnie shook his head slowly. "I told you. Not gonna happen."

"But every man has his breaking point," Ralph said. "You watch. Someday Slade's gonna open his mouth one too many times, and *bam!* Wolfe's gonna knock him clean into next week." He sat back, a wistful expression on his face. "Man, I just hope I'm around to see it."

Wendy looked at Ramona questioningly.

"They've got a bet going," Ramona told her. "Ralph is banking on the fact that someday Wolfe is going to snap and Slade will be eating dirt. To tell you the truth, I wouldn't mind seeing that myself."

"So you don't think much of Slade," Wendy said.

"Nope."

"If you don't like him, why don't you tell him to get lost?"

"Because every once in a while he brings somebody in. He does it recklessly, and sooner or later he's going to get his head blown off, but that's his problem. If he brings in a bail jumper, I pay him. If he's bleeding in the street because he was a careless idiot, I don't pay him. Simple as that."

"Is Rico really dangerous?"

"Yes."

"And Slade's going to bring him in?"

"He'll probably give it a shot. But I'm certainly not count-ing on it."

"But he said—"

"He said all kinds of things to impress you. Making money is fine, but Slade's number-one goal is to convince women how cool he is. Wolfe's goal is to get the bad guys off the street. And just for the record, Slade was full of crap about Rudy Pagliani. He was a bad one. The cops struck out, so Wolfe tracked him down and brought him in."

"So if the time comes with Rico, and Slade has struck out—"

"Then Wolfe will haul him in for me."

"You sound absolutely certain of that."

"His track record speaks for itself. Slade is hit-and-miss, and eventually he'll get himself into trouble. Wolfe works smart and gets results. In the end, which man do you think I depend on?"

Wendy had already suspected there was a lot more to Wolfe than met the eye, but now she was sure of it. All at once she felt a newfound admiration for him and an enhanced contempt for Slade.

"But I still don't understand," Wendy said. "Wolfe could flatten Slade in a heartbeat. So why does he take all that crap from him?"

"Get to know him a little better and you'll know why," Ramona said. "You'll know."

WENDY CAME THROUGH the door that evening to find Wolfe crashed out on the sofa reading. His bookshelves contained everything from classics to horror fiction to police procedurals to coffee-table volumes of twentieth-century architecture. She didn't know if he actually read all that stuff or not, but he was obviously engrossed in the mystery novel he was reading right now.

"You read a lot, don't you?" she asked him as she closed the door and locked it behind her.

"Passes the time."

She glanced up at the industrial fluorescent fixtures overhead that cast such a garish glow around the apartment. How he could read in this light, she'd never know.

"This light has got to be bad for your eyes," she told him. "Ever thought about getting a lamp or two?"

"Nope." He turned down a page of the book, then sat up and tossed it onto the coffee table. "Pizza's in the kitchen."

"Good. I'm starving."

Wolfe rose from the sofa, moving, as he always did, with a rough-around-the-edges kind of grace that mesmerized her.

"Any problems with the Chevy?" he asked, removing the pizza box from the oven.

"No. Why?"

"Transmission needs an overhaul, but it should be good for a little while longer."

"So does this mean I can drive it tomorrow, too?"

He opened the box. "How else will you get to work?"

Wendy smiled to herself, feeling those warm fuzzies stirring all over again.

"Oh," Wolfe said. "I almost forgot. Your mother phoned this afternoon and left a message. She said your sister told her what happened, but she just wanted to make sure you're all right."

"Yeah, I figured she'd call. I'll talk to her later." She paused. "Uh...how long should I tell her I'll be here?"

"How long do you think it'll take you to get the money you need?"

"I don't know," she said tentatively. "Maybe as long as a few months." She held her breath, waiting for his response.

"Just tell her she can get in touch with you here for the time being," Wolfe said.

Okay. He wasn't exactly saying she could stay forever, but he didn't freak out when she said a few months, either. That was a good thing.

She grabbed plates and forks and they sat down at the table. The smoky smell from last night had almost faded away, replaced by the aroma of a really nice deep-dish pepperoni pizza. Wendy lifted a piece, trailing a mile of stringy cheese behind it. She twisted her finger around it, then deposited the cheesy lump on top of the pizza.

"So did you have a nice day?" Wendy asked.

"Nice?"

"Yeah. You know. Did good things happen?"

Wolfe shrugged. "It was about like most."

"You have a pretty exciting job."

"Yeah. Exciting. Searching for addresses. Looking through public records. Calling every relative, friend or enemy a guy's ever had, trying to track him down. Looking for somebody with a vendetta who can't wait to blow the whistle on him. Chasing a dozen dead ends. Yeah, it's exciting, all right."

"I wouldn't exactly call my new job exciting, either," Wendy said, "but it wasn't bad at all. I like Ramona a lot."

"Yeah. She's a good person."

"She likes you, too."

"We go way back."

"Do you work for other bondsmen, too, or just Ramona?"

"I work for others, too. Whoever's got work at the time. But I always make sure Ramona's covered."

"How did she come to own a bail bond agency? I mean, I'm all for woman power, but it's still kind of unusual."

"She inherited it when her father died."

"Oh, yeah? How long ago was that?"

"Eleven years. She took it over when she was twenty-three."

Wendy blinked with surprise. "You're kidding."

"Nope. It was shaky there for a while, but she managed to hang on. Now she has a thriving business."

"How about Ralph and Lonnie? How long have they been there?"

"They worked for Ramona's father."

"How did they feel about a twenty-three-year-old girl taking over the business?"

"Not too good. But it wasn't long before they had to admit she could handle it. Now there isn't anything the two of them wouldn't do for her."

"Tell me about Slade," Wendy said.

Wolfe froze, the piece of pizza he held hovering in midair. "You need to stay away from him."

"Oh? Stay away from him? Why is that?"

"Because he's not the kind of guy you want to have anything to do with."

"Really?" she said innocently. "He's very handsome, you know."

Wolfe dropped the pizza back to his plate. "So that's all you look for in a man? A pretty face?"

"Well, of course not. But he is impressive in other ways. With those dangerous fugitives he goes after, and all."

Wolfe's eyes narrowed. "He's a risk taker who doesn't even belong in the profession. He's also a jerk who treats women like crap. He always has been, and he always will be."

She blinked with feigned surprise. "Really?"

"Damn it, Wendy! Are you that blind? Can't you see what kind of guy he is?"

Wendy nodded thoughtfully. "Actually, the moment I met him, I knew exactly what kind of guy he was. See, he made me think about a camping trip I went on once."

"What?"

"I was walking through some tall grass, and a snake slithered across my shoe. It was a very pretty snake, but a snake just the same."

Wolfe's expression went blank for a moment, and then annoyance seeped back in. "That's exactly right," he said sharply, yanking up his pizza again. "He's a snake. That's why you need to stay away from him."

He took a grinding bite of the pizza as if to say *Case closed*, and Wendy had to suppress a smile. As if she hadn't already figured Slade out five seconds after meeting him.

She rested her chin on her hand and smiled at Wolfe. "Thank you."

Wolfe paused midchew. "For what?"

"For looking out for me."

He actually looked a little flustered for a moment, then reverted to his annoyed expression. "God knows somebody has to," he muttered, then chomped into his slice again.

Wendy certainly hadn't expected this. When Wolfe was in the office today, he hadn't acknowledged that Slade even existed, but he sure was acknowledging him now.

Wait a minute. Yes, he had. The minute Wolfe had heard Slade talking about taking her out to dinner, he'd interrupted to tell her what was on the menu at his apartment that night.

As Wendy turned that thought over in her mind, she felt little tingles of delight. The subtext was suddenly so clear that she couldn't believe she hadn't seen it before: *Back off, buddy. She's with me.*

Maybe Wolfe was doing more than just tolerating her after all.

"Just for the record," Wendy said, "I don't find guys like Slade the least bit attractive." She paused. "Well, maybe if I saw his picture in a magazine or something, I might say *wow*. But the minute he opens his mouth..." She crinkled her nose with disgust. "All that conceit is compensating for something. I just don't know what. Any ideas?"

Wolfe shrugged. "Got me."

"Hmm." Wendy tapped her finger against her chin thoughtfully. "Small penis, maybe?"

Wolfe's eyes snapped up to meet hers, and for the first time since he'd picked her up on that icy street two nights ago, his mouth quirked into a smile. Then it grew broader. Finally it became a full-fledged grin, and Wendy couldn't believe how the sight of it made her feel—as if the clouds had parted and rays of sunshine were streaking down to earth.

"You're smiling," she said. "Are you sure you want to waste all that energy?"

"Sorry," he said, still grinning. "But I just got a visual on that. Can't help it."

"You mean you think it's *funny* that Slade has a tragically teeny weenie?"

Wolfe tried to bury his smile by covering his mouth with his hand, but still she could see it hanging on. Then he actually laughed a little, and the subsequent grin lit up his whole face, adding friendly little crinkles around his eyes and mouth. And it positively entranced her.

"You need to do that more often," she told him.

"What's that?" he asked.

"Smile."

He stared at her, his broad smile slowly fading to a softer one, and Wendy thought her heart was going to leap right out of her chest. Finally he looked away, rubbing his hand over his jaw.

"What's the matter?" Wendy asked. "Pull a muscle?"

He shot her a look of mock disgust.

"Don't worry," she told him. "It gets easier with more workouts. No pain, no gain, right?"

Wolfe let out a weary sigh. "You never let up, do you?"

"Nope. We'll have another session tomorrow. Maybe

hogging the bathroom, sitting on his end of the sofa or, God forbid, trying to cook again. It had everything to do with the fact that suddenly there was a beautiful woman moving around his apartment who smiled and laughed and drew him into more conversations than he'd had in the past five years, who filled up the empty spaces around him that he hadn't even realized existed. Ten minutes hadn't gone by all day when he wasn't thinking about her, and he knew just how dangerous that was. He'd spent his entire adult life perfecting the art of playing solitaire, and in just a few days she was already making him forget how to be alone.

This isn't forever. She'll be gone soon. Don't you ever forget that.

When he swung his SUV into its parking place he saw the Chevy there, which meant Wendy was already upstairs. She'd called him on his cell phone a few hours ago to tell him that she'd found a coupon for a fast-food chicken place in the newspaper so she'd pick up dinner for them on the way home.

Dinner waiting. That felt good.

Wendy waiting. That felt even better.

He went up the elevator and into his apartment, breathing a sigh of relief at finally being home. Then he looked into the living room, and he was stunned at what he saw.

Wendy was curled up on one end of the sofa, Weenie on the other. Neither of those things were unusual, except that his sofa now sat on a rug—a big fluffy beige-and-green rug. And there was a floor lamp beside the end of the sofa where he always sat to read.

"Well?" she asked. "Do you like it?"

He just stood there, staring at the incongruous sight: the soaring loft ceiling and cold brick walls juxtaposed with the pleasant glow that the lamp cast over the whole space, highlighting the softness of the rug, the relaxation of the cat and the warmth of the smile on Wendy's face.

"Here," she said. "Try it out."

She jumped up from the sofa, pulled off his coat, then took his hand and sat him down on the end of the sofa nearest the lamp. She put a newspaper in his hand.

"Go ahead. Read a little. You'll see how much nicer it is now than with those awful fluorescent lights."

He glanced down at the paper. He didn't see the words. Didn't care about the words. He just looked at the way the light shone on the page. Then he raised his head and noticed the way the light shone in Wendy's eyes.

"Weenie even appears better in this light," Wendy said. "And he needs all the help he can get."

Wolfe glanced at the cat, who had twisted around to lie upside down with his paws sticking up in the air. "He looks like roadkill."

"Ah, but now he's *well-lit* roadkill."

"Where did you get this stuff?" Wolfe asked.

"Shame on you. You're not supposed to ask where gifts come from."

"I thought you were saving money."

She sat down next to him, tucking her legs beside her. "I am. But Ramona gave me an advance on my salary today, and I thought these things would be nice."

"But they must have cost a lot."

"Not when you shop at the Trinity River Thrift Store. Hope you don't mind that they're a little bit used."

No. He didn't. Not in the least. The items themselves didn't matter at all, because it wasn't about those.

It was about Wendy.

She got up suddenly, shoved the coffee table out of the way, then sat down cross-legged on the rug. She ran her palms over it, closing her eyes with delight. Then to his surprise, she yanked her sneakers off, then her socks. She put her hands behind her and rested on her palms, then brought her knees up and dug her toes into the deep pile of the rug.

"It feels really soft," she murmured. "Wanna try it?"

"No, thanks."

"Oh, come on. Take off your shoes and socks."

Before he realized what was happening, she'd grabbed his right foot and yanked off his boot.

"Wendy!"

She tossed the boot aside and grabbed his other one, tugging it off, too, then went for his socks. He pulled his feet away. "Will you cut that out?"

"Oh, just be still, will you?"

She shoved one leg of his jeans up and pulled the sock down, wincing when she caught sight of his bruised shin.

"Ooh," she said. "Bad bruise. What happened?"

"A young lady expressed dismay that I was returning her to jail today."

"I hope that was the low point of your day."

"Not by a long shot."

"Ah, then. All the more reason to relax."

She peeled off both of his socks, then stopped again, staring with surprise. "Damn, you have big feet."

"You expected them to be small?"

"Good point." She came to her knees, took his hands and tugged.

"What are you doing?" he said.

"Will you just come down here?"

He sighed with resignation and slid off the sofa to sit on the rug beside her.

"This is stupid," he muttered.

"No. You'll love it. I promise. Stick your toes in the rug and wiggle them around."

Good Lord. If the criminal element of the city of Dallas

could see him now, his career would be over. He rolled his eyes, then buried his toes in the deep pile of the rug.

"See?" she said. "Soft, huh?"

He turned to stare at her. "Yeah. Soft."

He wasn't lying. Everything about her was soft—her hair, her eyes, her voice. The rug could have been soft, too, for all he knew, but he couldn't have focused on it right now if his life depended on it.

He leaned back against the sofa, crossing his ankles in front of him. Wendy did the same, pulling her knees up and wrapping her arms around them. Until this moment when he saw the infusion of warmth that came from the rug and the lamp and from Wendy herself, he hadn't realized just how cold and uninviting this place really was.

"So what else happened today besides getting your shin kicked?" she asked him.

"Well, let's see. A drug dealer I was chasing down skipped the country, and while I was handcuffing a teenage burglary suspect, he peed all over himself."

"You're kidding."

"Wish I were. It was a real red-letter day."

She gave him a sympathetic smile. "Don't worry. Tomorrow is bound to be better."

"Don't bank on that. You know the kinds of people I deal with."

"Yeah. That's an interesting profession you've got there. How did you end up as a bounty hunter?"

"Ramona hired me when I was eighteen."

"And you just started doing the job?"

"Pretty much. How about you? You want to be an actress. Where did that come from?"

"Well, first of all, I just wanted to get out of Glenover, Iowa. It's the kind of place that's good to be *from*."

"What's wrong with it?"

She shrugged. "Nothing, I guess, as long as you don't mind working in a gum factory."

"Gum factory?"

"Yeah. As in chewing gum. It's where my parents work. And my brothers and sisters and just about everyone else in Glenover. My father got me on there right after my high-school graduation. I'm the fifth child, so by the time my turn came, working in the factory was a family tradition. I hated every minute of it."

"A lot of people these days are just happy to have a job."

"Not me. I'd rather die than be tied down to a place like that for the rest of my life. Ever work on an assembly line?"

"Nope."

"Boring. Mundane. One face in a crowd of thousands. It's horrible. But it's what almost everyone in Glenover does."

"Only, you wanted to be an actress."

"Yeah. It all started when I was in a play in high school. I loved it. I couldn't get it out of my mind, especially when I stood on an assembly line for eight hours every day. So one day I took my life's savings, packed up everything I owned and headed to New York."

"But that didn't work out."

"It's like I told you. In New York theater, there's only so far you can go so fast. So after beating my head against that wall for a few years, one day I thought, *Hey, stupid! What are you doing here? You should be in Hollywood!* So off I went."

"And then you got sidetracked in Dallas."

She smiled. "Yeah. Just a little. But that doesn't mean I've taken my eyes off the prize." She held up her palm. "But I'm not delusional, either. I'm certainly not expecting to get any major roles right off the bat. But I promise you that one of these days, my face is going to be on the cover of *People* or *Entertainment Weekly*. That's my benchmark. That's when I'll know I've made it."

"You sure are aiming big."

"That's my motto. Go big, or go home."

"And home's not an option."

"Exactly. But it's never going to come to that. I'm a pretty good actress, and I've got the right look. Almost, anyway. And some people say my smile is just like Julia Roberts's. That can't hurt, right? If I add big boobs and blond hair, I've got a shot at the big bucks. It's the Hollywood formula."

"So where are you hiding yours?"

"What?"

"Your big boobs and your blond hair."

She waved her hand. "Oh, I can get those. All it takes is money. My dark hair is a big handicap, but that's what a good salon is for. To take up the slack where nature blew it."

He wondered where she'd come to the conclusion that nature had blown anything where she was concerned. That gorgeous dark hair flowed over her shoulders like a sheet of rainwater, and the very thought of attacking it with chemicals made him cringe.

"There are brunette actresses," he said.

"Sure. I could make it with this hair. But I'll make it faster as a blonde."

"Your eyes are dark brown. That's gonna look funny."

"Nah. As long as my hair's blond, my eyes could be purple for all anyone cares. But if it becomes an issue, there are always colored contacts."

Wolfe couldn't help looking at the second part of the equation, the one she was a little shy on. As soon as his attention slid south, she cleared her throat.

"Up here, Wolfe."

His gaze shot back up, and she rolled her eyes. "*Men.* They think we don't see them staring, but we always do. And the answer to your question is *breast augmentation.*"

He blinked with surprise. "You're kidding."

"Nope. I lie down on the operating table. When I wake up, instant sex appeal. Small price, big rewards." She paused. "Well, it's not a small price, I guess."

That was when he knew. "So that's what the five thousand dollars was for."

"Yes."

He made a scoffing noise. "Then you're lucky it was stolen. You look fine."

"Oh, come on! Why do men do that? They say, 'Oh, no, honey. I like you just the way you are,' and then when a double-D walks by they can barely stuff their eyes back into their heads."

"You don't need double-Ds."

"Oh, yeah? You see two women. The one has brown hair, and her chest looks like the plains of West Texas. The other one is a blonde with boobs the size of the Goodyear blimp. Which one attracts you the most?"

He pondered that for a moment. "Is either one of them naked?"

She let out a breath of disgust. "Go with me on this, will you?"

He shrugged. "You can ask all day long, but it's still no big deal to me. Just keep what nature gave you."

"Hey, the other day you thought I ought to have bigger breasts. *Way* bigger."

"You were playing a hooker!"

"Well, then, you just made my point. That's what it takes to attract men. Big breasts. Ninety-five percent of men love them, and the other five percent are liars."

"I *told* you it doesn't matter to me!"

She smiled. "Welcome to the five percent."

"Okay!" Wolfe said, throwing up his hands. "You're right. I admit it. I lied. Yes. I love big breasts. I stare at them constantly. I'm a knuckle-dragging Cro-Magnon with no control over my own eyeballs and I think all well-endowed women should walk around topless just to entertain me. There. Are you happy?''

She sat back with a big grin. "Why, Wolfe. Such sarcasm. I didn't know you had it in you."

He gave her a mock glare of disgust. "You drive me to it."

"I drive you to sarcasm?"

"Actually, that's the very *least* of what you drive me to."

She turned and propped her arm on the seat of the sofa beside his shoulder and rested her chin on her hand, her broad smile becoming warm and engaging.

"Tell me what else," she said softly.

She looked at him as if there were a hundred different meanings to her words, and he had no idea what to say. He'd spoken the truth. She'd driven him to all kinds of things. To look at himself, at the place he lived, at the life he led, and realize that maybe something was lacking.

Or someone.

She looked so beautiful sitting there next to him that his power of speech had completely deserted him. Her slight, willowy figure always seemed as if it was blowing in a gentle breeze. For a split second he imagined making love to her, but she seemed so fragile that he'd be terrified of hurting her.

No. That would never happen. If fate ever chose to smile on him like that, he'd be so damned careful, always aware of how big he was and how big she wasn't. But it was the body she had right now that he wanted to touch, not the chemically and surgically altered one she swore was in her future.

"With this acting thing," he said, "have you thought about just being yourself?"

"You're different for your job. Why shouldn't I be?"

"What are you talking about?"

"You play a real badass."

"No playing there, sweetheart."

"Yeah, okay. I can see how you might fool some people. But I know better, don't I?"

Her gaze remained fixed on his. Those dark eyes stared at him without blinking, and he had the most unsettling feeling that she could see right inside him. Then all at once she reached up and touched his cheek, tracing her fingertip down the length of that awful scar.

"What happened here?" she asked.

He turned away quickly, wishing to God she wouldn't focus on that. "Gang fight."

"You were in a gang?"

"No. I was trying to stay out of one."

"When was that?"

"When I was sixteen. One of the gangs in the neighborhood where I lived thought they could use a guy like me."

"A guy like you?"

"At sixteen, I wasn't much smaller than I am now. They needed some muscle and wanted me to provide it."

"What happened?"

He really didn't want to talk about that. It wasn't a memory he cared to relive in any way, but Wendy just sat there, calmly staring at him and waiting for him to continue.

"They cornered me one day for a recruitment party. They offered me all kinds of things to join them, from drugs to women to God knows what else. I told them to forget it and got up to leave. They had other ideas. And that was when the fight started."

"Sounds as if you were lucky you got out alive."

"Probably."

"Did they bother you any more after that?"

Wolfe felt a sudden coldness in the pit of his stomach. He hadn't thought about all that for a long time, filing it away in the back of his mind under the heading of *History*. But now he was stabbed by the memory all over again, how he'd been caught between looking like a bad guy and trying so hard not to become one.

"Yeah," he told Wendy. "They bothered me. But it wasn't anything I couldn't handle."

"But you were just a kid. You shouldn't have had to deal with that."

"Where I came from, you grew up fast."

"But what about your parents? Couldn't they do something?"

Wolfe shook his head. "My father was long gone. My mother worked all the time just to put food on the table. My brother and I were pretty much on our own."

"You have a brother?"

"Yeah. He's three years younger than I am."

"Where is he now?"

"In Houston. He just opened a dental practice."

"Your brother is a dentist?"

"Don't sound so shocked."

"It's just that you seem to have chosen different paths."

"He had the brains, I had the brawn. You don't fight nature."

"Do you ever see him?"

"Sure. My mother lives in Houston now, too, so I see all of them on holidays. David has a nice wife, nice family."

"Why don't you?"

"Why don't I what?"

"Have a nice wife and a nice family."

Wolfe felt a shiver of longing at the very thought of that. It wasn't something he allowed himself to dwell on very often, but every once in a while when it was just him alone in this apartment staring at four walls, he thought about his brother and his wife, and he wondered how the years had passed and he'd ended up here instead of where he really wanted to be. But he knew the answer to that. When a nice woman pictured the kind of man she wanted to marry, a man like him never came to mind.

"I don't know," he told Wendy. "I guess it was just never in the cards."

"Maybe someday, huh?"

"Yeah. Maybe."

Wendy nodded, then focused on his scar again, her voice dropping to a near whisper. "I'm glad you told them to go to hell. I'm just so sorry they hurt you like that."

When Wolfe saw the expression of pity on her face, it made him feel uglier than he ever had in his life.

"It's no big deal, Wendy."

"No big deal?"

"What difference does a scar like this make when you've got a face like mine?"

She blinked. "A face like yours?"

He turned away. "You know what I mean."

"No," she said softly. "I don't think I do."

She continued to stare at him until he faced her again. She lifted her hand, this time resting her palm against his cheek. She leaned in closer to him, so close he swore he could feel her warm breath quiver in the air between them. Then, to his utter amazement, she touched her lips to his, sweetly, tentatively. Every nerve in his body came alive, his heart pounding wildly.

She backed away a few inches, her expression earnest and sincere. "Please tell me that was a good thing to do."

That she even had to ask the question astonished him. That she appeared to wonder what his answer might be astonished him even more. The moment her lips met his, it was as if the black-and-white canvas of his life had exploded into brilliant color, and all of it was because of Wendy.

He slowly lifted his hand and smoothed it along her shoulder to the side of her neck, then slipped it beneath her gorgeous cascade of hair to rest against the back of her neck. She was soft and sweet and felt like heaven, a dazzling thing of beauty in his stark, isolated existence.

''It was a good thing to do,'' he told her, then pulled her forward and kissed her.

10

THE MOMENT WOLFE'S MOUTH fell against Wendy's, she felt a flood of excitement that it was finally happening, that he was finally kissing her, that finally she could touch him the way she'd so desperately wanted to.

In those few moments right after she'd kissed him, he'd stared at her, his eyes wide, the air between them quivering with invisible question marks, and she thought for sure she'd done the wrong thing. But then he kissed her, gently at first, then more insistently, and all those question marks had vanished. The slick, wet heat of his tongue against hers felt wonderful, and she returned his kiss with an intensity that astonished even her. But this was the man who'd filled her mind with delicious thoughts since the moment she'd met him, and she absolutely couldn't get enough.

He cradled her head in his hand and tilted it back, dragging his lips from her mouth to her jaw, kissing her there, then easing them over to her neck, where he pressed one kiss after another, adding tiny nips at her earlobe that sent hot shivers sizzling through her whole body. He pushed her shirt aside to kiss the curve of her neck where it met her shoulder, then returned his lips to hers and kissed her endlessly until she almost couldn't breathe, until she felt as if she was drowning in him.

And suddenly kissing wasn't enough.

With a single gasping breath, she tore away, rose to her knees, slipped one leg over him and straddled his lap, her palms resting against his shoulders. He tensed with surprise, but she immediately dipped her head to kiss him, and a second later she felt his big hands wrap around her thighs. He stroked them up and down, before moving to her hips and her waist and back down to her knees again in a deep, delicious massaging motion that made her whole body go limp with pleasure.

Then he eased his thumbs over to stroke the crevice between her thighs and hips. She sat up straight. Gathering the shoulders of his sweatshirt in her fists, she took a deep breath of ecstasy and let it out slowly.

More. She had to have *more*.

Still gripping his sweatshirt, she pulled herself forward and whispered in his ear, "I'm sorry I almost saw you naked that morning."

"You're forgiven."

"Good. Then maybe you won't mind getting naked now."

His hands froze on her thighs. She sensed his surprise, but if he was going to object he'd have to do it in a hurry, because she'd already grabbed the hem of his sweatshirt and was yanking it upward. Thankfully, he caught it on the way up and pulled it over his head, revealing that beautiful chest to her for the first time since the morning when she'd nearly fainted from the sight.

As she slung his shirt down to the rug beside them, he was already tugging her shirttail out of the back of her jeans, and a second later, his cold hands lit against her bare skin. She gasped, laughing a little. He whispered an apology and moved his hands over her back, up and down and in big sweeping circles until they were as warm as she was, and she couldn't help arching against him because it felt so good.

"Mmm," he said. "No bra."

"You noticed."

He slipped his hands from beneath her shirt, bringing them around to the front to cradle her breasts in his palms. Wendy felt a shot of self-consciousness. They were small enough as it was, and in Wolfe's big hands she knew they'd seem even tinier still, but then he was rubbing her nipples and strumming them with his thumbs. Even through her shirt they were growing hard and tight and agonizingly sensitive and she forgot all about her embarrassment and leaned into him, asking for more. As if he'd read her mind, he reached to the collar of her shirt and unfastened the first button.

Yes.

He was moving fast but not fast enough, so Wendy undid the bottom button, ascending as he descended, and when they reached the middle, she dropped her hands, allowing him to unfasten the final button. Slowly he spread her shirt open.

He stopped. Stared. Wendy watched him watching her, and all at once self-consciousness overtook her again. She grabbed the edges of her shirt and tried to pull them together again, but he took hold of her wrists and held her in place.

"No, sweetheart, no," he said quietly. "Don't do that."

"I'm still not sure you like what you see."

"Oh, I like it. Believe me."

Slowly he opened her shirt, watching intently as her breasts came into view again. He circled his hands around them.

"Don't you let anyone change these," he said. "Ever."

"Can't promise that."

"I swear I'll beat the hell out of any plastic surgeon who lays a hand on you."

He passed his thumbs over her nipples, and she closed

her eyes and drew in a small, blissful breath. "You know, I think I'm actually starting to believe you."

"I mean what I say. Always."

He moved his hands down to her waist and pulled her forward, kissing the space between her breasts, then tracing his tongue around her nipples, first one, then the other. The feeling was so intense all she could do was clutch his shoulders, gasp for air and hope she didn't pass out.

Beneath her she felt the expanse of his muscled thighs and his erection straining against his jeans. She eased forward a little and shimmied her hips, pressing herself against him. She couldn't believe how hot and wet she felt already, as if she was melting from wanting him so much, and she kept moving because she just couldn't *not* move. As she bore down on him harder, a groan rose in his throat, a deep, masculine sound of utter satisfaction.

Then all at once he grasped her by the waist, stilling her. He squeezed his eyes closed and held his breath for a moment before letting it out slowly. "Easy, sweetheart. You're inciting a one-man riot here."

"That's kind of what I was hoping for."

He sat up suddenly, and before she knew it, he'd pulled her off his lap and lowered her quickly but gently to her back on the rug. She felt a little swoop in her stomach that multiplied deliciously when he moved between her legs, towering over her. He stared down at her, his eyes full of wicked intent.

"What now?" she said, raising an eyebrow, daring him to make his next move.

"I want to see what you look like naked on the new rug."

Wendy blinked slowly with delight, loving the sound of his voice. It was so strong, so powerful, so full of desire, and it made her want him *now*.

She smiled at him. "So I guess it's not so bad having me around after all, is it?"

Wolfe's expression faltered. "Of course it's not."

"You didn't say that a few days ago when I burned a certain dinner." She gave him a provocative smile. "But don't worry. I think you'll like me a lot better in the bedroom than you did in the kitchen."

Wolfe went completely still. "What did you say?"

She started to tell him that it was quite simple, actually. That she did her best cooking *without* pots and pans. Then she saw his eyes narrow with suspicion at the same time his mouth turned down in an angry frown.

"Wendy?" he said sharply. "What are you doing?"

Confused, she sat up slowly, pulling one of her legs over his and tucking it in front of her. She reached for him, but to her dismay, he slid away from her and stood up.

"Wolfe?"

He picked his shirt up off the floor and yanked it on over his head, tugging it down to his waist.

"I was already going to let you stay longer. You don't have to give me sex to make that happen."

For several long, shaky moments, all Wendy could do was stare at him, speechless, certain she couldn't possibly have heard him right.

"What in the hell are you talking about?"

"You get free food, free rent, and all you have to do is bring me a few cheap gifts and put out a little. No big deal, right?"

Her mouth fell open. "You think that's why I wanted to do this? So you'll let me stay?"

"You said it yourself. 'You'll like me a lot more in the bedroom than you did in the kitchen.' So what's the deal, Wendy? If one manipulation doesn't work, try another one?"

She stood up, yanking her shirt closed, her stomach turning over with disbelief. "That's *not* what this is about!"

"Right."

His challenging expression filled her with desperation. Yes, she'd spoken those words, but she hadn't meant them like that. She'd only been teasing him, just as she'd teased him about a hundred other things. Couldn't he see that?

Her heart felt as if it were crumbling, and she couldn't stop tears from filling her eyes.

Wolfe made a scoffing noise. "Come on, Wendy. Cut out the tears. Do you really think I'm going to fall for that again?"

"You're twisting everything around!"

"Actually, I think I'm finally straightening everything out." He brushed past her and started toward his bedroom.

Wendy grabbed his wrist. "Wolfe, please don't."

He pulled his wrist away. "You know what? It's my fault for being such an idiot. I should have known something was up. After all, you're a beautiful woman. And beautiful women don't just throw themselves at a man like me."

He strode down the hall and into his bedroom, slamming the door behind him.

Stunned, Wendy just stood there, staring at the closed door, the echo of it still reverberating through the room. How could he have done this? How could he have suggested that she had a list of ulterior motives a mile long, when nothing could be further from the truth?

Suddenly she was right back to feeling the same way she had that first night—cold and lost and desperate—only now it was so much worse because she knew what warm and safe felt like. Her anger at him for hurling those accusations when she'd done nothing to deserve them didn't begin to match the pain she felt that he'd ever believe such a thing about her in the first place.

She sat down on the end of the sofa where Wolfe usually sat. It was now bathed in lamplight, and she wondered how it was possible to feel so warm on the outside and so cold on the inside. She kept asking herself why he had done this and could come up with no answer at all.

WOLFE TOOK OFF his sweatshirt again and threw it on top of his dresser. He paced back and forth a few times, then walked over and sat down on the end of his bed.

He held out his hands. They were shaking.

He dropped his head to them and ran his fingers through his hair, squeezing his eyes closed, feeling as queasy as if he had a case of the flu.

He felt angry. Humiliated. That was why his stomach was all tied up in knots. He'd learned early in his life that if something seemed to be too good to be true, it probably was, so he should have spotted her true intentions at ten paces. Since they hadn't talked about how long she could stay, she was undoubtedly thinking that he was going to kick her out at any moment, and she wanted to make damned sure that didn't happen.

I think you'll like me a lot better in the bedroom than you did in the kitchen.

How stupid could he possibly have been?

Suddenly he was assaulted by images of the beautiful women he'd admired from afar over the years, the ones who'd looked away from him the second their eyes met. He'd gotten to the point where he wouldn't even try to strike up a conversation with a woman he didn't know because of the look that always came into her eyes. The one that said hell would freeze over before he'd ever lay a hand on her.

Then Wendy had shown up in his life. She had looked him right in the eye, smiling, laughing, seeming to want him with a kind of intimacy that had given him hope, acting as if the gentlest touch from him was like heaven to her. For a few brief minutes tonight he'd been deluded enough to think that had meant something. Now he knew the truth. She *was* a good actress. After her performance tonight, he had no doubt she'd be a star, right after she screwed up her body with big breasts and blond hair and all that other crap that no self-respecting woman would ever consider doing to herself.

He felt angry at being used. So damned angry.

Then cynicism crept in. Maybe he'd been stupid to push her away. After all, if she wanted to sleep with him, what difference did it make what her motives were? He should have just said thanks for the gifts and had hot, screaming sex with her on that rug and considered himself lucky. A nice tradeoff, right? She'd have a place to stay, and he'd have a warm body in his bed. He'd had plenty of sex in his life just for the sake of sex, so what was wrong with doing it this time?

He dropped his head to his hands again, knowing the answer to that question.

Because this time, with Wendy, he'd wanted so much more.

11

WHEN WENDY WOKE the next morning, a few moments passed before she remembered what had happened between her and Wolfe. She turned over and looked at the clock on the coffee table. It was just after seven. What was she going to do now?

With the advance on her salary Ramona had given her, she could afford a cheap hotel for a day or two. But how she'd get to work, she didn't know. And she had no idea what she'd do when her money ran out.

She sat up slowly and looked around the apartment. Hopefully Wolfe had left already and she would be spared having to deal with him. She could sit down, have a cup of coffee and think about what to do next.

She rose from the sofa and went down the hall, surprised to see his bedroom door still closed. Then she went to the kitchen and saw his car keys lying on the counter.

Damn. He was still here. And the worst part of it was that she was caught in the middle of that one nonnegotiable necessity that was going to force her to have to talk to him.

She went back to his bedroom and knocked on his door.

"Go away," he shouted.

"I have to get into the bathroom," she called out.

There was a long silence.

"Come in."

With a deep, nervous breath, she opened the door, intending to ignore him completely and walk straight to the bathroom. But then she glanced over to see him lying on his back, blankets pulled up to his waist, his arm resting on his forehead and his eyes closed.

"Make it fast," he muttered in a harsh, raspy voice.

Wendy stopped. Stared at him. "Wolfe?"

"I said move it."

She came closer to his bed. "What's the matter?"

He moved his arm and looked up at her. His face was drawn and tight, his eyes droopy. His skin was uncharacteristically pale, but his cheeks were flushed red.

"You're sick," she said.

"I'm fine."

But as he put his forearm back over his eyes, she saw his chest rising and falling with increased respirations, as if he truly was in pain. She stood there a moment, unsure what to do, but eventually the sight of this tough-as-nails man so ill displaced her anger enough that she eased over to his bed and sat down beside him.

"Wendy. Go away."

She rested her palm against his cheek. It was on fire. "You've got a fever. Are you sick to your stomach?"

He pulled his forearm away from his eyes and put his palm against his stomach with a shaky sigh.

"Looks like the flu," Wendy told him.

"Yes. I've got the flu. Now will you just get out of here and let me die in peace?"

"You shouldn't be alone when you're this sick."

"It wouldn't be the first time. I can manage by myself."

"Do you have any medicine?"

"I don't know."

"Food you can eat that won't make you even sicker?"

"I don't know."

"I'll go to the grocery store."

"No! Damn it, I don't need you!"

She gave him a stern look. "Listen up, Wolfe. In spite of the fact that you were such a jerk last night, I owe you a lot. I'm not about to leave you here alone when you can't even lift your head off the pillow."

"Wendy—"

"Get well first, and then we'll talk. Right now it wouldn't be a fair fight."

She rose from the bed, then turned back and pointed a finger at him. "And if you think I'm doing this just so you'll let me stay here longer, you're dead wrong, so don't even go there."

He covered his eyes with his arm again. She had no idea whether he believed that or not, but she wasn't going to worry about it now. She went to the bathroom and got dressed. Then she grabbed the keys to the Chevy, told Wolfe she'd be back in thirty minutes and left the apartment.

NOW WOLFE KNEW why he'd felt as if he had the flu last night.

Because he did.

He didn't get sick often, but he remembered the last time with painful clarity. He'd felt positively wretched for three days, hot and restless and hungry because he had so little food in the house and he couldn't bear to get out of bed to go get any. It had been a good thing that he'd been too weak to lift a gun to his head or he'd have probably just put himself out of his own misery. But even that paled in comparison to the way he felt now, so by the time Wendy returned from the grocery store half an hour later with chicken soup, bananas, rice, applesauce, flu medicine and aspirin, he was well on his way to wishing he were dead.

"What about your job?" he asked when she came back into the room.

"I called Ramona and told her you were sick. She said you

probably picked up something from her. Doesn't she ever stay home sick?"

"She hasn't since I've known her."

"Lonnie told me yesterday that she's had everything but the bubonic plague."

Bubonic plague. Maybe he could catch that. It was bound to be an improvement over the way he felt right now.

"If you stay here," Wolfe said, "you'll get what I've got."

"Not a chance. I come from a family of eleven. I've been exposed to so much stuff that I've got antibodies against every germ on the planet."

Wendy sat on the bed and put her palm on his cheek again, pursing her lips with concern. She made him drink some liquid that was supposed to help relieve the flu symptoms, then draped a cool washcloth on his forehead.

"Wendy, you don't have to—"

"Don't give me a hard time about this, Wolfe. You're in no condition to argue."

He closed his eyes, the cool washcloth countering some of the heat radiating from his body. No matter how much he protested, it felt good. It was embarrassing to be so weak and helpless, but Wendy hovered around him as if it was no big deal, and eventually he gave in and let her do whatever she wanted to, never asking for her help but never turning it down, either.

Over the next several hours she changed that washcloth about fifty times so it would always be cool. She fixed him chicken soup and toast and bananas and cups full of ice chips, telling him that those were things that even she couldn't screw up and that he wouldn't *throw* up, encouraging him to eat when he didn't think he'd ever be able to face another bite of food as long as he lived. She turned on the portable TV in his bedroom and handed him the remote. He kept telling himself that no matter what she'd said, she'd do anything to have a place to stay and that was why she was helping him. But he couldn't shake the feeling that when she touched him, it felt like so much more.

He dozed off and on most of the day, flipping restlessly in bed as the buzz of news and talk shows droned in his ears, feeling calm only when Wendy came in periodically to bring him medicine and something to eat. Late that evening he fell asleep, and when he woke, his room was dark. He figured she must have shut off the TV and the lights before going to bed herself. He rolled over, his stomach still in turmoil, sweating and feeling chilled at the same time. His clock said two-twenty.

He collapsed against the pillow again. Just then the door of his bedroom squeaked open and Wendy appeared in the doorway. She wore one of his shirts, its tail grazing the back of her knees. Light from the room beyond the door placed her in near-silhouette.

"Did I wake you?" she asked.

"No. I was awake already."

"Your fever was high when I went to bed. I woke up and thought maybe I'd better check on you."

She came into his bedroom, and he felt that heavenly little dip in his mattress as she sat down. He let out a silent sigh of pleasure at the feel of her cool palm against his face, wishing he could take her hand and hold it there forever.

"Your temperature is still high," she said. "I'll get medicine."

She went into the kitchen and brought him aspirin and water. He downed it, then lay back against the pillow again.

"Is there anything else I can get for you?" she asked.

You, he thought. *That's what I want. What I need. That's the only thing on this earth that will make me feel better right now.*

"No," he said. "Nothing."

She rose from his bed and went to the door. When she

turned back, the light from the other room formed a warm aura around her.

"Call me if you need me."

Wendy slipped away, closing the door behind her, leaving him in darkness once again.

THE NEXT MORNING, Wolfe told Wendy he felt better, and this time it wasn't a lie. But better than death still wasn't great, and getting out of bed was pretty much out of the question. When he mentioned that daytime television bored him to tears, she asked if he wanted a book to read, but he still felt too sick to focus on the words.

To his surprise, she retrieved the mystery novel he'd bookmarked a few nights ago and began to read to him instead. He started to tell her it wasn't necessary, but the actress in her came out from the first sentence she spoke, and he could tell she was actually having a good time playing all the characters. Most of the time he couldn't concentrate enough even to comprehend what she was saying, and of course her running commentary on who she thought the murderer was more or less screwed up the whodunit experience. But her voice, so soft and sweet, filled the silence, making him forget his body aches and his pounding head and his jumbled-up stomach.

But as the day wore on, he thought about the accusations he'd thrown at her. Doubt began to crowd his mind, followed by a sense of shame that made him feel even worse than his flu symptoms did. When she looked at him, it wasn't carefully calculated premeditation he saw in her eyes, but genuine concern. And that drew him to a conclusion he hadn't wanted to face: maybe she'd been telling him the truth the other night. Maybe she really had wanted to make love with him. And if that were true, then the things he'd said to her...

Tell her you were wrong. Tell her you're sorry.

He wanted to say the words, but he just couldn't do it, because he still had that deep-seated doubt in the back of his mind that told him that if he did, somehow the joke was going to be on him. It wouldn't be the first time in his life that wishful thinking had led to a wake-up call that had taught him to be even warier than before, and he knew he couldn't bear it if it happened again.

He slept away most of the afternoon. When evening came, Wendy brought him dinner. After he ate, she took the dishes to the kitchen and then returned, asking him if he needed anything else. When he said no, she started to leave the room.

"Wendy?"

"Yeah?"

"It's almost seven. One of those weird reality shows is coming on."

"Yeah?"

"Why don't you stay for a while?"

She froze, clearly a little surprised. "You hate those shows."

"I know. It'll probably only make me sicker. But..." He paused. "Just stay. You know. If you want to."

He pulled up a pillow beside him and rested it against the headboard in silent invitation. She came forward tentatively and climbed onto the bed. He handed her the remote. She looked at it as if it had fallen from the moon.

"You're giving me the remote? Are you too weak to push the buttons?"

"Better enjoy it while you can."

She flipped to the show. It turned out to be every bit as stupid as Wolfe had imagined it would be, but Wendy's comments about the people involved kept it from being deadly dull. And when it was over, she switched to a cop drama, telling him it was only fair.

They watched that show for the first fifteen minutes, and then a commercial came on. Wendy muted the sound. "How are you doing? Can I get you anything?"

"No. I'm fine. Are you sure you're not a nurse in disguise?"

"Like I said, I come from a family of eleven. Somebody was always sick. I might not have been able to cook, but I could do the nurse thing."

"Division of labor?"

"It was the only way to get everything done. Everybody had their jobs, like cogs turning a wheel."

"Must have been something having a family that big."

"Yeah, it was something, all right. One more crowd to get lost in. Most of the time I just felt invisible."

"Invisible?"

"Yeah." She pondered that for a moment. "It felt so weird sometimes. As if I was right there in the room, but nobody could see me. I'd sit at the dinner table sometimes and think that there was such a crowd around the table that if I just didn't show up one night, it might take them a couple of hours even to realize it. I know that sounds strange that I could have so many people around and still feel alone, but that's the way it was."

She stared straight ahead, an uncharacteristically dark expression on her face, and for the first time Wolfe got a sense of the child she must have been—surrounded by so many people yet never feeling as if she belonged.

Then she smiled. "But when I was a senior in high school, I had the lead in those plays I told you about." She settled back against the pillow, a faraway look on her face. "That curtain would go up, and for those few hours, hundreds of people were watching every move I made. Hanging on every word I said. They put my picture in the newspaper. Friends and family sent me flowers. People stopped me in the hall at school and told me how wonderful my performance was. I loved it. For once in my life, *everybody* knew I existed." She turned to face him. "That seems silly and shallow to you, doesn't it?"

"No," he said, and meant it. "Not the way you say it."

"It's okay if you think so, because sometimes it sounds that way even to me. But then I think back to the summer following my senior year when my father got me on at the factory. I thought I'd died and gone to hell. Working there made me feel even more invisible, because I went from being one out of eleven to being one out of a thousand. Sometimes I felt as if I was slowly fading away, and one day I'd disappear altogether." She sighed. "That's my biggest fear, you know."

"What's that?"

She turned her head on the pillow with an earnest expression. "Making no mark. Having my life be like a rock that falls into a pond but never makes a ripple. I had a dream one night that I died and my headstone was blank. Not a solitary soul knew or cared that I had lived or died. But if I'm famous, the whole world will know me. I'll have one of those great big funerals that everybody comes to and people I don't even know are boo-hooing because I'm gone. That would *really* be something."

Wolfe winced. "How about we don't talk about your dying?"

She grinned. "But that's when you know whether you've really made it or not. When you die."

"I'd like to argue with that logic, but I'm still not a hundred percent here."

"I'm just making a point." Her voice quieted again, this time full of emotion. "I'm going to be famous, Wolfe. Someday the whole world is going to know my name. You just watch me."

The look on her face was so uncharacteristically intense it took Wolfe by surprise. And all at once he realized the most startling truth.

She was lonely.

Outside she was a beautiful, energetic, confident woman, but inside was a little girl who was screaming to be singled out from the crowd, screaming for somebody to say she was special. When she was on stage she felt that high for the first time, and now she craved it over and over. He only hoped that if she ever got what she wanted, it really did make her happy.

They watched the rest of the cop show, but as the minutes passed, Wendy's eyes grew heavy. By the end of the episode, in spite of all the gunfire and the sirens and the nonstop shouting, she'd fallen asleep, one hand tucked beneath her pillow and the other hand clutching the remote. The collar of the shirt she was wearing rested halfway down her upper arm. Her dark hair spilled over her shoulder, a striking contrast to the pale expanse of her neck and upper chest.

God, she was beautiful.

For the longest time he just lay there staring at her, watching the rhythmic rise and fall of her chest and the brush of her dark lashes against her cheeks. Finally he slipped the remote out of her hand and clicked off the TV. The moment the sound disappeared, Wendy opened her eyes. She rose suddenly, sitting up and blinking sleepily.

"Sorry," she said. "Just closed my eyes for a minute. Guess I fell asleep. Better go to the sofa."

She started to get up, but Wolfe caught her arm. "Is it more comfortable here than on the sofa?"

She blinked sleepily. "A bed of rocks would be more comfortable than the sofa."

"Then stay."

He fixed his gaze on hers without wavering, reinforcing his invitation. She didn't say anything. Instead, she merely turned and flipped out the lamp, then settled her head back against the pillow. Wolfe lay down beside her, and her hand crept over to rest against his arm.

"Wolfe?"

Her voice sounded so sleepy that he knew she was barely awake. "Yes?"

"What we did that night..."

His heart skipped. "Yes?"

"I wanted you. So much. That's the only reason I wanted to make love with you. I just can't bear to have you think anything else."

He started to respond, but then she closed her eyes with a soft sigh, and seconds later her rhythmic breathing told him she'd fallen asleep again.

"I know, Wendy," he whispered, brushing a strand of hair away from her cheek. "I know."

WHEN WENDY WOKE UP the next morning, she glanced beside her, surprised to see that Wolfe wasn't there. Then she heard the muffled sound of shower spray.

She closed her eyes again, knowing she should still be angry at him. After the terrible things he'd said to her, she should be storming out the door as soon as he was well. Instead, her anger had disappeared completely, and the fight she'd promised him when he got better had simply melted away into nothingness.

A few minutes later the shower fell silent. Soon Wolfe came out of the bathroom, wearing nothing but a pair of jeans. His dark hair was slicked back, and he'd just shaved. For the first time in two days, color had returned to his face.

She smiled. "You look better."

"I feel better."

"Come here."

He walked over to the bed and sat down. She placed her palm against his forehead, then his cheek. "No fever."

She let her hand linger there a few seconds too long and saw the shift in his expression that told her he'd recognized that fact. She still wasn't sure what he believed about her motives and what he didn't, so she pulled her hand away. For all she knew, now that he was better, he was going to tell her to leave. She felt a flutter of apprehension at the thought. As of right now, she had absolutely nowhere else to go. But the truth was that whether she had a place to go or not, this was the place she wanted to be.

Before he could say the words she didn't want to hear, she slipped out of bed and told him it was her turn in the shower. On her way to the bathroom, she stopped at his dresser. As she'd done every day while she was here, she removed the bracelet she wore and laid it on the dresser, then swept her hair to one side and reached up to unhook her necklace.

At that moment, she glanced in the mirror and saw Wolfe rise from the bed. He came up behind her. Taking the necklace from between her fingers, he unfastened it, his fingertips brushing the nape of her neck, then lifted it off over her head. He refastened it and laid it on the dresser, then circled his arms around her, engulfing her in a warm embrace, his lips only a scant inch from her ear.

"Thank you for taking care of me."

Wendy's heart skipped crazily. She hadn't expected this. She hadn't expected him to hold her so close, to speak so softly, and she scarcely knew what to say.

"I just couldn't bear the thought of you being here sick and alone," she told him. "Not after everything you've done for me."

His lips fell against her neck, kissing it softly. "Is that the only reason you did it?"

As Wendy realized what was happening, she felt a surge of exhilaration. She closed her eyes and brought her hands up to grasp his forearms, drawing in his clean, fresh, masculine scent, reveling in the feeling of being in his arms again.

"No," she said. "I did it because I wanted to be here. With you."

He dropped his hand to her waist, flattening his palm against her stomach. He eased her back against him, and when he spoke again she felt his warm breath against her neck.

"Other women," he said. "The way they look at me sometimes. Or don't look at me. It's been that way since I was thirteen years old. And then you came along. So bright, so beautiful, the kind of woman who can have any man she wants. So I just didn't understand why in the hell you wanted me."

Suddenly Wendy remembered the clerk's reaction at the thrift store, when she'd looked at him as if he intended to rob the place. When they'd gone to the grocery store that first night, a woman stocking the shelves had watched every move he made, as if he was getting ready to shoplift something. Wendy had seen firsthand exactly what he was talking about, and it angered her to think that people had judged him that way his entire life.

Then she felt a surge of shame. After all, hadn't she reacted that way herself the night he'd first picked her up? Hadn't she accused him of being a rapist and a murderer, mostly because of the way he looked? How must that have made him feel?

You're a beautiful woman. And beautiful women don't just throw themselves at a man like me.

As she remembered his words from two nights ago, she felt a sudden jolt of understanding. The moment he'd said that, she'd been focused only on the way she felt, so angry and hurt and...oh, *God*. How could she not have heard what he'd been saying?

He tightened his arms around her, touching his lips to the skin just below her ear. "The things I said to you the other night. I'm so sorry, Wendy. I just didn't believe...I couldn't believe..."

"Wolfe," she said softly, turning in his arms and staring up at him. *"Believe."*

She circled her arms around his neck and touched her lips to his in a gentle kiss. Then she pulled away slightly, staring up at him. Several seconds passed, the air between them growing hotter and heavier with every breath they took.

"You have no idea how much I want you," Wolfe whispered.

"Then maybe you'd better show me."

12

WOLFE SLIPPED HIS ARM around Wendy, pulled her right up next to him and kissed her with a sudden intensity that was so unexpected and so wonderful, she could barely catch her breath for the elation she felt. Five minutes ago, she hadn't been sure of anything where Wolfe was concerned, and now his mouth was moving against hers with the kind of mindless gotta-have-you passion that she'd been craving. Being held by a man of such overwhelming strength woke up something hot and exciting inside her, but she knew this same powerful man would beg forgiveness for the faintest bruise he might inflict on her. To feel so safe and so cherished made her knees weak with desire, and she vowed that this time absolutely nothing was going to come between them.

Before she could think straight enough to wonder what was coming next, he broke the kiss and swept her into his arms. To her surprise, he bypassed the bed and headed for the door, only to stop suddenly.

"Damn it."

He put her down. "Don't move," he said, then strode back to the dresser, yanked open a drawer and pulled out a condom. He started to shut the drawer, paused, then opened it again and grabbed two more.

Wendy smiled. "Ambitious, aren't you?"

He stuffed the condoms into his jeans pocket as he strode back toward her, then lifted her into his arms again. "No interruptions this time," he said, and carried her into the living room, where he lay her gently on the rug. Wendy's heart soared.

"You like your gift," she said.

"Yes. Especially when you're lying on it."

"Naked?"

"You're reading my mind, sweetheart."

Already he was tugging on her T-shirt. She sat up so he could pull it off over her head, her hair swooping through the opening. She'd barely lowered her arms before he was pressing her down to her back again and going for her panties. In moments he had them off.

He stopped. Stared. Then he stretched out beside her, resting on one elbow, and trailed his hand from her breasts to her abdomen and up again, watching what was passing beneath his hand with an expression of total appreciation. He pressed his hand to her breast, squeezing it softly, his calloused fingertips rasping gently across her skin. Then he strummed her nipple with his thumb, watching as it rose to a peak. Shivers of hot pleasure streaked through her, escalating wildly when he bent and passed his lips back and forth over her nipple, then closed his mouth over it and sucked gently. She writhed beneath him, but he placed a palm against her abdomen, stilling her, as he continued to tease her. Then he eased over to place a gentle kiss against her other breast.

"You're perfect just the way you are," he said, "Don't you ever forget that."

She knew he meant it. He truly did. And it astonished her.

"Your jeans," she said, barely able to speak. "Take them off."

She rose a little and tried to reach for the buttons, but he pressed her back against the rug and dipped down to give her a long, lazy kiss, followed by another, and another, each one blending into the last. At the same time he slipped his hand lower, smoothing it up and down one of her legs, over and over. She tried reaching for his buttons again.

"Wolfe, *please.*"

"Relax, sweetheart. We've got nothing but time."

"Fine. We can take all the time in the world once you're naked."

But all he did was smile at her, then lean in to kiss her, which was very, very good, but she wanted more. Way more. The only thing better than a gorgeous, bare-chested man in a pair of tight jeans was that same man *out* of those jeans.

"Wolfe?"

He kissed her again.

"Your jeans..."

When he ignored her and leaned in for yet another kiss, she ducked out from underneath him and sat up, giving him an admonishing look.

"Wolfe. I'm getting the feeling that you're not paying attention to me."

He drew back with an innocent expression. "Why, sweetheart, of course I'm paying attention to you."

"If you were paying attention, you'd be naked by now."

With a furtive smile, he rolled to his back and started to unbutton his jeans, but she pushed his hands aside and reached for the buttons herself. Once she'd undone them, she knelt between his legs and took hold of the waistband. She worked her way backward on her knees, pulling his jeans off as she went. And the moment she got a look at what lay beneath, she froze, staring at him in total awe. Then amazement.

Then anticipation.

"Well," she said, a little breathless, "I guess I should have expected it. After all, you do have big feet."

She pulled his jeans off the rest of the way and tossed them aside, then crawled forward again and slipped her palms from his knees all the way up his thighs to his hips and back down again. He closed his eyes with a sigh of satisfaction. As she continued to stroke him, his breathing escalated, his hands opening and closing in a slow, mindless rhythm.

"Oh, sweetheart, that's good," he murmured.

Good thing, because she loved touching him like this. She also loved the unexpected. In a flash of pure devilment, she dipped down and streaked her tongue right up the length of that amazingly large part of him.

His eyes sprang open. He sat up instantly and took her by the upper arms, then bowed his head and let out a long breath.

"Wolfe?" she said innocently. "Is something the matter?"

"You can't be doing that kind of thing. Not right now."

"You didn't like it?"

"Like it?" He gave her a strangled laugh. "Hell, yes, I liked it. And if you do it again, I'm going to have to handcuff you. Then comes the duct tape right over your mouth."

"Hmm. Kinky."

"Kinky, hell. It's self-preservation. I don't want this to be over with. Not just yet."

"Maybe next time?"

"Definitely next time. But for now—"

"Are you telling me that I can't even touch you?" She smoothed her fingertips down the length of his erection, then circled her fingers around it and stroked it once, twice—

He grabbed her hand and pulled it away, exhaling sharply. He spun around, fumbled for his jeans and shoved his hand into one of the front pockets.

"Condom," he muttered. "Where's a damned condom?"

Wendy smiled furtively. "I think you put them in the other pocket."

He stuffed his hand into the other pocket and fished around wildly.

"Wolfe," she said. "Relax. We've got nothing but time."

He shot her a look of disgust, then finally retrieved one of the little plastic packets. "There," he said on a breath of relief.

She took it out of his hand. "Okay," she said brightly. "Just lie back, and I'll—"

"No way," he said, yanking it right back and holding up his palm. "You stay away." He ripped the packet open with his teeth, then looked at Wendy a little sheepishly. "No offense."

Wendy smiled. "None taken."

In seconds he'd rolled the condom on, then lowered her to her back and rested on his elbow beside her again, stroking his palm along her cheek and kissing her gently. "Are you ready for me, sweetheart?"

"Touch me and find out."

With his eyes fixed on hers, he pressed his palm to her abdomen, then moved his hand lower, finally dipping his fingers between her legs, stroking there slowly. She was already so hot and slick that the slightest touch sent shivers radiating through her whole body.

"Yes," Wolfe murmured. "That's exactly how I want you."

She was dying for him to get on with it, but he kept touching her, teasing his fingers against the most sensitive part of her, his urgency transformed into a single-minded attempt to drive her crazy. Soon the random sensations began to narrow and coalesce, and she couldn't help moving against him, arching up to meet him as he stroked her. Her fingers tightened against the rug, and before long she had a death grip on the pile, her eyes squeezed closed.

"Enough," she told him breathlessly.

"Oh, yeah? Why is that?"

"For the same reason you wanted me to stop," she said, squirming beneath his hand.

"I thought you said we had nothing but time."

"Well, time's about to run out. Believe me. Where are those handcuffs?"

"Sorry, sweetheart. I'm in charge of those."

"First the remote, now the handcuffs. What do I get to be in charge of?"

"Absolutely nothing," he murmured, still caressing her. "I'm taking care of everything."

She opened her eyes and saw him staring down at her. She'd had plenty of sex in her life, but never had a man looked at her like this, as if she was the center of his existence, as if nothing else in the world mattered to him but being right here with her right now.

Then his expression grew somber. "I'm so sorry about the things I said to you the other night," he said softly. "I swear I'll never do anything like that again."

"Just make love to me. That's all I want."

He moved between her knees and rose above her, and her heart nearly exploded with anticipation. Resting his palms on the rug, he slipped inside her with a gentle thrust, and the sudden intense pleasure ripped a moan of satisfaction from her throat. Wolfe froze, holding himself motionless above her.

"Wendy? Am I hurting you?"

"Hurt? Oh, you have *got* to be joking." She took his face in her hands, stroking it with her thumbs to erase the concern she saw there. "The only way you can hurt me now is if you stop."

In spite of her eagerness, in spite of how wet and seemingly ready she was, still she sensed his restraint, his knowledge of just how big he was and how easily he could hurt her. But she knew he wouldn't. She knew he would control every move he made, protecting her from pain and giving her only pleasure, freeing her mind to relax and her body to let go.

He lowered himself to his elbows and began to move inside her, taking her with smooth, steady thrusts, which released tiny quivers of excitement inside her. He moved slowly, building incrementally, and she clutched his shoulders and curled her legs around him in a silent plea for more. With every thrust she seemed to open more to him, and he pressed on, deeper and faster, until the spark inside her began to catch fire. But still she felt his muscles clenching with the effort it took to hold himself back.

"More," she said breathlessly. *"More."*

"I don't want to hurt you."

"You won't. Just please...*please*..."

On his next stroke, she rocked her hips up hard to meet his, and on the next one, too, and the next...

"Easy, baby...take it easy..."

"No!" she said, pushing herself against him as hard as she could. "Wolfe, please...I want it...I want *you*..."

That was the moment his control snapped.

Slipping his arm beneath her, he buried his face against her neck and fell into a hot, intense rhythm, but she was so ready for him that there was no discomfort at all, only pleasure. For a few tense seconds the world seemed to contract around her, every molecule spinning tighter and tighter, and then...

Like the sudden flare of a torch, a scorching sensation swept through her. She gasped and gripped his shoulders, arching up to meet him.

"Wolfe...yes...oh, *yes*..."

As she shuddered beneath him, a groan rose in his throat, and he fell into her with even deeper, more powerful thrusts. She could feel his climax as surely as she felt her own, and she wrapped herself around him, clutching at him wildly as he surged against her, driving her from pleasure right into ecstasy. The feeling seemed to go on forever, hitting every nerve ending with electricity, then traveling to her mind to explode in bursts of light and color.

As the feeling wound down, Wolfe lay over her for several moments, his muscles quivering beneath her palms. Then he laced his fingers through her hair and kissed her lips, her cheek, her forehead. "You're incredible," he said breathlessly, and she hoped the fact that she could barely mumble a reply told him that she thought the same about him.

Finally he rolled to one side and pulled her along with him. She curled up in his arms, still breathing hard. She draped her thigh over his, and he ran his hand up and down it in long, soothing strokes. In unison, they each took a long breath and let it out slowly, then laughed a little at the unexpected harmony.

Being with Wolfe was so unbelievably good that Wendy thought she was still asleep and she'd dreamed the whole thing. But that wasn't true. He was real, he was here, and she didn't think she'd ever felt so content in her entire life. And then she had the most uncanny feeling that this *was* her life.

But that was crazy. Their paths had crossed only for these few moments in time, and soon they'd be going their separate ways again. So why did she feel as if she'd perish if she was more than a foot away from him, much less a thousand miles away in Los Angeles?

No. Don't think about the future. Think only about what's right here and right now.

For the rest of the day they stayed in bed, touching, sleeping, making love. Evening came, and they ate enough to keep body and soul together, then went back to bed again and watched only half of something dumb on TV before they were making love all over again. Later that night, after they'd turned out the lights and were on the verge of sleep, Wendy reached up and stroked Wolfe's cheek. He opened his eyes.

"There's something you never told me," she whispered.

"What's that?"

"Your first name."

He paused. "Michael."

"Michael," she repeated, trying it out.

There was a long silence.

"It's just nice to know," she said. "But I think you'll always be Wolfe to me."

THE NEXT MORNING, Wendy woke early. She took a shower, got dressed, then came back and sat down on the bed beside Wolfe, waking him with a gentle kiss. He blinked his eyes open, and a look of distress came over his face.

"Hey," he said, as if he barely recognized her with clothes on. "What's this?"

"If I stay away any longer, Ramona's liable to fire me. How are you feeling?"

"Good enough to take those clothes right off you again."

"Sorry. Can't go to work naked."

"But you can stay here naked. Come here."

He took her by the hand, pulled her back and kissed her, and it was all Wendy could do not to hop right back into bed with him.

"What are your plans today?" she asked.

"I think I'll stay close to home. Make some phone calls. Do a little computer research."

"Then you'll be here when I get home tonight?"

"Yes. I'll be here."

She smiled. "I can't wait."

She gave him one more quick kiss, then rose from the bed. He settled back down to the pillow. She'd just about made it to the bedroom door when he called out to her.

"They keys to the Porsche are on the kitchen counter."

She froze, then turned back with a look of utter astonishment. "You're letting me drive your Porsche?"

"I'm worried about the Chevy's transmission. You might get stranded."

"You might, too."

"I'll drive the SUV."

She just couldn't wipe the surprised expression off her face. Clearly the pod people had removed the real Wolfe in the middle of the night and put a car-indifferent version in his place.

"Uh...sure," Wendy said. "Okay. Yeah. I guess I can drive the Porsche. Any special instructions?"

Wolfe settled back against the pillow and closed his eyes. "You wreck it, you die."

Wendy smiled and slipped out the door.

13

IT WAS UNCHARACTERISTICALLY warm for a February morning, so Wendy tossed her purple coat into the back seat of the Porsche before climbing inside, smiling the whole time. Traffic was sparse. She made every stoplight. The Porsche drove like a dream. By the time she arrived at the office, she was still smiling. Driving a really hot car did that to a girl.

Oh, hell. Who was she kidding? It was sleeping with a really hot man that did that to a girl.

A few minutes later, when she was making a pot of coffee, she just couldn't help humming. Then singing. She stuck the filter in the pot with a little flourish, then measured out the right amount of coffee. She poured the water to the tune of "Singing in the Rain." By the time she flipped the machine on, she'd moved on to "Oh, What a Beautiful Morning," because it was. A *very* beautiful morning.

Ramona appeared at the doorway. "Show tunes," she deadpanned. "My favorite."

Wendy wiped a few granules of coffee off the counter with a damp paper towel.

"So what's up with you?" Ramona asked.

"Nothing," Wendy said, smiling a little on the outside and a lot on the inside. "I guess I just felt like singing."

"Was I seeing things, or is that Wolfe's Porsche out in the parking lot?"

"Yes. It's Wolfe's Porsche. Hot car, huh?"

"Come on, Wendy. What's up?"

There was no way she could hide it. The silly grin on her face gave it all away.

Suddenly Ramona's eyebrows flew up. "Oh, my God."

"What?"

"You're glowing."

"Glowing?"

"You know what I mean."

Wendy tried to suppress her grin, but it just wasn't happening. "Oh, okay. So I'm glowing."

"Does this mean you and Wolfe—"

"Now, come on, Ramona. I'm not one to kiss and tell."

Ramona walked over and pulled a chair away from the table. "Sit."

Wendy rolled her eyes. She poured each of them a cup of coffee and brought them to the table.

"Okay," Ramona said. "Last I heard from you, Wolfe was sick."

"He got better." She smiled. "*Way* better."

"Oh, yeah?" Ramona sat back in her chair with a satisfied expression, sipping her coffee. "That's good."

One of these days, if Wendy stayed around here long enough, she was going to be able to figure out what Ramona was saying even when she wasn't saying it.

"You know, he tries to act so tough," Wendy said. "But that's not really who he is at all, is it?"

"No. It's not. But most women don't come to that conclusion."

"Maybe they should look a little deeper."

"Yeah. They'd find out all kinds of surprising things." Ramona tapped her fingertips on her mug. "Wolfe came to work for me right after I took over this business. Did he ever tell you how that happened?"

"No. Not exactly. He said he was eighteen when you hired him, but that was about it."

"It's an interesting story." Ramona set her mug down on the table. "When he was growing up, the neighborhood he lived in started out nice enough. Then it got taken over by a really bad element. Drug dealers, prostitutes, gang activity."

"Gangs? Wolfe told me that was how he got that scar. He said they hassled him a lot, but it wasn't anything he couldn't handle."

"Oh, he handled it, all right."

"What?"

"One day one of those guys stepped over the line."

"What do you mean?"

"There was a drive-by shooting at Wolfe's house. A bullet went right through the living-room window. It was meant for him. It got his brother instead."

"His brother, David? The one who lives in Houston now?"

"Yeah. It put him in the hospital. It was touch-and-go for a while, but he recovered. Wolfe knew who did it. He told the police. But days passed, and they still hadn't picked the guy up. Wolfe even saw him on the street a few times and tried to get the police out there to do something. Still nothing. Then one day he had enough."

"What did he do?"

"He grabbed the guy, dragged him down to the police station, slammed him down on the sergeant's desk, and said, '*There's* your drive-by shooter.'"

Wendy's mouth fell open. "You're kidding."

"Knowing Wolfe, do you really doubt it?"

She didn't.

"Anyway," Ramona went on, "word got around about this guy who'd done the police's job for them. I went to talk to him. He was an eighteen-year-old boy with the body of a heavyweight prizefighter, and I admit he scared the hell out of me the first time I saw him. But when he told me what had happened with his brother and why he dragged that guy to the police station...well, let's just say I knew he was the kind of man I wanted working for me."

Wendy was astonished. Wolfe had mentioned his relationship with his brother, but she had no idea they had a history like that.

"Wolfe isn't close to many people in this world," Ramona said. "But when he loves somebody he loves them fiercely. And he takes care of them."

"His brother?"

"Yeah."

"You?"

Ramona smiled a little. "In a different way, but yeah. It was tough when I took over this business from my father. But even in the beginning, when Wolfe was barely an adult, he helped me every way he possibly could. He's the one person I know I can always count on."

"So have you and Wolfe ever...?" Wendy looked at her pointedly. "You know."

She shook her head. "No. It's never been like that between us."

"Have you ever thought about it?"

"Thought about it? Sure. I guess so. But sometimes people come into your life who are just meant to be friends. He means a lot to me, Wendy. I'm just so afraid sometimes that he's going to stay holed up in that weird apartment of his, and then one day he's going to turn around and wonder where his life went. And he's too good a man for that." She paused. "But then, you know that, don't you?"

She did. And suddenly she felt a little stirring of something she hadn't counted on. Something that went beyond the fun and excitement of the past twenty-four hours and edged right into respect and admiration and attraction of an entirely different kind, the kind that made her heart race with the desire to see him again.

Ramona rose from the table. "I have to head over to the courthouse. You and the boys hold down the fort until I get back."

After Ramona left the office, Wendy said hi to Ralph and Lonnie and got to work. Unfortunately, she was absolutely certain that her daydreaming was going to leave her seriously unproductive. Then somebody walked through the door who interrupted both her work and her daydreaming, and she resented the hell out of it.

Slade sauntered over, sat down in the chair in front of her desk and put one booted foot against the edge of it. She was surprised to see a large bruise on his forehead in several shades of black-and-blue. She thought about asking him which woman had finally gotten fed up with him and smacked him one, then decided she really didn't give a damn.

"Hey, baby," he said.

"Foot off the desk."

Slade slowly withdrew his foot and sat up. "You're looking good today." He sniffed the air. "What's that perfume you're wearing?"

"Extrastrength deodorant."

Wendy pulled a pair of files out of her desk drawer and laid one open on her desk. Slade slumped back in the chair again, folding his arms across his chest.

"You sure do play hard to get."

"Try impossible to get."

"Wrong. I never say never."

"Do you have a purpose for being here other than to harass me?"

"Yeah. Actually, I do." He tossed a bail ticket down on her desk. "I got Rico."

Wendy picked it up, staring at it with surprise. Now she knew why his face looked like a human punching bag.

"You're kidding," Wendy said.

"Nope. There it is in black-and-white."

"Actually, it's on your face in black-and-blue. Did the going get a little tough?"

"I told you already. It's a dangerous business. Sometimes I have to take a few hits."

"One of these days you're going to take a few bullets."

"No way, baby. Not me. I'm always on top of things." He casually pushed his jacket aside, revealing a shoulder holster containing a very large weapon, clearly a piece of above-the-waist equipment to compensate for his lack of below-the-waist equipment.

"You'll have to wait to get your money until Ramona gets back," she told him.

"Whatever." He leaned forward again and rested his arms on her desk. "So how about it? You and me. Tonight. A bottle of champagne and a nice, soft mattress. What do you say?"

"No, thank you."

"But I'm hurting here, baby. I had to take a few punches just to get that guy off the street." He leaned in and spoke seductively. "I could use a little TLC right now."

"Sorry, Slade. I have plans."

He sat back with a look of disgust. "Oh, come on, Wendy. Don't tell me that you and Godzilla are still an item."

A slow burn of anger flared inside her, nearly driving her to blacken the other side of Slade's face.

No. Don't waste the effort. He's not worth it.

"I just don't get it," Slade said. "What in the hell do you see in him?"

"Sorry. I don't have the time to read that list to you. But the next time I have a free hour, I'll give you a call."

"Next time you have a free hour, I'll take you to heaven."

"In that case, I'd prefer hell."

Lonnie and Ralph snickered. Slade gave her a face-saving I-don't-give-a-damn look, then stood up slowly, placing his palms against her desk.

"The day's going to come when you want a real man. And when it does, you'd just better hope I'm still available." He stood back up. "Tell Ramona I'll be back in a few hours."

As he turned and walked out of the office, Wendy gritted her teeth, thinking he should consider himself lucky she didn't kick his butt all the way down the block.

Ralph turned to Lonnie. "I've got twenty bucks that says Wendy decks him before Wolfe does."

"Ha!" Lonnie said. "I'm not touching that one. I might as well hand you twenty bucks."

Ralph gave a low whistle. "Between the two of them, Slade's days are numbered." He sat back in his chair with a wistful expression. "Whenever it happens, I just hope I'm around to see it."

As THE DAYS PASSED, Wolfe found it hard to remember what life without Wendy had been like. She was there most evenings when he came home, greeting him with something marginally edible she'd cooked for dinner, and then they'd spend the evening relaxing in front of the television or reading or just talking.

And then they'd go to bed together.

She'd insinuated herself into every facet of his life, filling in blanks he never knew he had, making him feel alive in a way he never had been before and pushing the memory of his once solitary existence far to the back of his mind.

As the days turned into weeks, she even began helping him with his work. In her spare time, she began cruising through Ramona's files, looking for situations where she thought she might be able to help track somebody down. Skip tracing—knowing where to look, who to talk to and what to say when you got somebody on the phone in order to find out the necessary information—was almost an art form, and Wendy was a natural.

The moment she picked up the phone, the actress in her came out, and she could tell the little white lies that were sometimes required to extract information even Wolfe couldn't get. She even started logging on to his computer at home, searching through public records to help him put two and two together to find a bail jumper's whereabouts. In a few weeks, she gave him details he could use to help locate people he might not have found otherwise. In light of that, he really shouldn't have been surprised when she wanted to jump into yet another aspect of his job with both feet.

He came home one afternoon, intending to pick up a quick bite to eat before heading out for surveillance that night. He'd told Wendy that morning that he'd be away most of the evening. She'd seemed so disappointed that he almost relented and told her he'd skip it, but he had a line on a guy he'd been after for a while, and it was time he brought him in. Not a big apprehension, but it was the routine ones that kept money in his pocket. Yes, it would be a screaming bore, but a necessary one. Then he got home and found out it wasn't going to be as boring as he thought.

Wendy wanted to come with him.

"Go with me?" he said. "What for?"

"To keep you company."

"You don't want to do that. Believe me."

"Why not?"

"Because there's nothing on earth more boring than a surveillance. I found out where his girlfriend lives, and I'm just hoping to get lucky and he'll show up there. I could be sitting there for hours for nothing."

"Then you ought to be happy that I want to come along and keep you company. As a matter of fact, I've packed some snacks in case we're out there for a while." She picked up a paper bag off the kitchen table and opened it up. "See, it's all here. Apples, granola bars, pretzels, those cheese crackers you like, Twinkies for my sugar fix and bottled water. You bring the binoculars and the handcuffs, and we're all set."

"Wendy, I don't think you understand just how boring—"

She dropped the bag, circled her arms around his neck and silenced him with a kiss so scorching it could have brought a dead man back to life. It was all he could do not to strip her naked right there.

"Granola bars, you say? Are they the chewy ones with the chocolate chips?"

"Yes."

"Okay, then. You can come."

14

JOE DIXON WAS the kind of criminal who really had no reason to jump bail. He was a low-level drug dealer who would probably get off fairly easily if his attorney had any sense at all, but still he hadn't bothered to show up to court. One of those not-too-bright criminals who practically demanded that revolving doors be put on courthouses.

Wolfe pulled his van up near the house in question and killed the engine. He got up and moved to the back. Wendy followed.

"Cool van," Wendy said, looking around at his surveillance equipment, then running her hand over the bunk at the back of the van. "Nice place to crash. Do you sleep here often?"

"Only if I get dragged out of town on somebody's trail. Saves having to get a hotel room if it's just one night."

"Okay. Tell me what's going on with this guy."

Wolfe pointed out the window. "Dixon's girlfriend lives in that house across the street two doors down." Wolfe sat on the bunk, picked up the binoculars and zeroed in on the house in question. "I've got a source who says Dixon is hot for her in a major way. Chances are he won't be able to stay away for long."

"Can I see?" Wendy asked.

Wolfe handed the binoculars to her, then swapped places so she was sitting in front of him on the bunk.

"Okay," she said. "I see the house."

"Can you see through the window?"

"Yeah. There's a woman inside. She's dressed to kill. All made up. Looks like she's waiting for a hot date. Dixon?"

"Let's hope."

"Okay, now she's sitting down on the sofa. Grabbing the phone. Calling...calling...ooh. She looks a little pissed. Wonder if he stood her up?"

Wendy looked back over her shoulder at Wolfe with a calculating smile. "A woman scorned is a woman who'll get her boyfriend's butt over to her house no matter what. This should be good."

As Wendy looked through the binoculars again, Wolfe wondered if there was anything that Wendy undertook that she didn't have a good time doing, if there was any way to dampen the good spirits that radiated from her twenty-four hours a day.

If he was going to be able to keep his mind off her beautiful body long enough to get this job done.

He sat so close behind her that he could smell the last traces of the flowery shampoo she'd used that morning. The collar of her sweater had slid to one side, and he stared down at the curve of her neck as it sloped along to her shoulder. Suddenly, surveilling Dixon was the last thing on Wolfe's mind.

He pushed the sweater to the edge of her shoulder, then leaned in and kissed it.

"What are you doing?" she asked.

"Surveillance."

"Wolfe," she murmured, staring through the binoculars again. "We have to keep watch."

"I am watching."

"Watching me doesn't count."

"Okay, then. Let me have the binoculars."

She handed them to him. He immediately tossed them

aside. Without missing a beat, he reached for the hem of her sweater and pulled it up, forcing her to raise her arms as he slid it off over her head.

"Wolfe! What are you doing?"

He tossed it down on top of the binoculars. "There. That's better."

She started to turn around, but he put his hand against her shoulder.

"Nope. Don't move."

He took his shirt off, then edged closer to her, pressing his chest to her back. He circled his arms around her, then closed his hand over her naked breasts and squeezed softly.

"You're playing on the job," Wendy said.

"Nah. I'm the boss. I'm giving myself a break."

Wendy sighed softly, relaxing against him. "This is how you expect to make a living? Feeling me up in your surveillance van?"

"Okay. So it doesn't pay much. But the perks are unbelievable."

All at once Wendy sat up straight. "Oh! Oh! Wolfe!"

"What?"

"Dixon!" she said, pointing out the window. "Is that him?"

He teased his lips over her neck. "What?"

"I see...see a car pulling up to the house..."

He smoothed his hands down until one palm lay flat against her stomach and the other moved up and down her thigh. "A car?"

"Yeah," she said, a little distracted. "And a man...is getting out...and..."

"A man?"

"Yes. Dixon. It has to be Dixon."

Wolfe nudged her hair aside with his lips and nipped her earlobe, still stroking her thigh. "Don't care."

"But your bail jumper—"

"Forget him. Low-end. Nonviolent. Dime a dozen."

"Don't you want to apprehend this guy?"

Wolfe dragged his lips across her cheek. "Guy? What guy?"

Wendy laughed softly. With a faint groan of resignation, she dropped her head back to rest against his shoulder.

"Okay," she said. "I give up."

"You're so easy."

"No. You're just persuasive."

She turned around and he dragged her into his lap, kissing her hard and deep as he cradled her in his arms. She was so beautiful, so willing, and he was so incredibly hot for her. All he wanted in this world was to make love to her right here and right now. He lay her down on the bunk and reached for the top button of her jeans. Just the sight of her half-naked filled him with anticipation, so he could only imagine how he was going to feel when she was *totally* naked. He flicked the button open. Then all at once, Wendy put her hands down on top of his.

"Uh-oh."

"What?"

She stared up at him, her eyes wide. "I don't suppose you brought a condom, did you?"

As the implication of that little omission made its way to Wolfe's sex-heated brain, he muttered a curse. Not once in his career had he ever had occasion to use a condom on a surveillance, but why hadn't he anticipated that this surveillance just might be a little different than most?

"Please tell me you have one in that sack of yours," he said.

"Sorry." She paused. "How about an apple instead?"

Wolfe rose from the bunk.

"Where are you going?" Wendy asked.

"Home."

She reached for her sweater. Before she could grab it, he yanked it up and headed for the front of the van, depositing it in the front passenger seat on top of her coat.

"Hey! What are you doing?"

"Saving myself some time later."

"But—"

"We're only five minutes from home. Just sit there and think about what I'm going to do to you when we get there."

"So I'm just supposed to sit back here half-naked?"

"That's the plan." He started the van, then glanced into the rearview mirror. "Move a little to your left."

Confused, she did as he asked, crossing her arms over her breasts at the same time.

"Nope," he said. "Arms down."

She placed her palms against the seat.

"Ah, there you go," he said. "That's perfect. Now, stay exactly in that position until we get home."

She drew back with feigned offense. "Hey! What do you think I am, anyway? Your own personal sex toy?"

"Works for me."

"Pervert."

"Exhibitionist."

Wendy looked at him admonishingly. "You are *so* bad."

"Just enjoy the ride, sweetheart," he told her, shoving the van into gear. "I know I'm going to."

After pulling onto the street, he glanced into the rearview mirror, surprised to see that Wendy's expression had shifted from a narrow-eyed glare to a speculative look. She picked up the sack she'd brought and pulled out an apple. She sniffed it sinfully, then took a bite, chewing on it slowly.

"Mmm. I do love apples."

Her voice had slipped into a lower register, deep and

throaty. Seductive. She took another bite, blinking with delight.

What in the hell was she doing?

Then, to his utter disbelief, she sat back on the bunk and, beginning at her navel, she ran the apple slowly back and forth over her stomach. Back and forth. Back and forth.

"How about you, Wolfe?" she said, meeting his eyes in the mirror. "Do you like apples?"

"Uh...they're okay."

He flicked his gaze from the road to the rearview mirror, watching as she moved the apple upward to her breasts, rubbing the fruit in circles around her nipples, then dragging it right across them. She smiled seductively.

"Do you like them any better now?" she asked.

Oh, hell, yes. If she'd been holding a kumquat it would instantly have become his favorite fruit of all time.

She closed her eyes with a rapturous sigh. "Mmm. Now I know what Eve saw in apples."

Suddenly Wolfe realized that his attention had lingered in the rearview mirror a few seconds too long. He glanced back at the road again.

Curb. *Damn.*

He yanked the wheel hard to the left, causing the van to lurch. One more second looking in that rearview mirror, and he'd have been cruising down the sidewalk.

"Wolfe," Wendy said admonishingly. "You keep your eyes on the road, now. Don't you go getting us into an accident."

Okay. So this hadn't been such a smart move after all. What good did it do him to look at her naked if he ended up wrapping the van around a telephone pole?

"Once Eve ate the apple," Wolfe said, "she had to get dressed." He grabbed Wendy's sweater and tossed it to her. "Time for you to do the same."

"Throw me a fig leaf," she said, flinging the sweater right back, "and I might."

Damn.

A few minutes later, he entered the warehouse and wheeled the van into its parking place. He leaped out of the vehicle and grabbed her sweater and his coat, leaving his shirt behind. He tossed her sweater onto the hood of the SUV beside the van. As he circled around to the back door of the van, he put on his coat, then opened the door to find her fumbling around, apparently looking for the sweater he'd deposited outside the car. She wheeled around to face him.

"Hey! What did you do with my sweater?"

He leaned in and gave her a look of warning. "I'll teach you to tease me."

She crawled up on the bunk by the back door. She met him eye to eye, giving him a smug smile. "Excuse me, Wolfe, but I think I already know how."

Before she realized what was happening, he grabbed her and hoisted her over his shoulder. He slammed the door behind him and started for the elevator.

"Are you *nuts?*" she shouted. "It's freezing out here!"

"You'll be warm soon enough. I'll make sure of that."

He carried her through the warehouse, reaching into his coat pocket with his other hand to grab the remote for the elevator. He hit the button, and by the time they reached it, the doors had opened.

He walked in, set her down and, as the doors were closing, he pressed her against the wall of the elevator. When the cold metal met her bare back she yelped and jumped forward, rubbing up against him. He backed her against the wall again, pinning her hands at her sides and kissing her long and hard. She smelled like apples. Felt like heaven. As he kissed her, she seemed to dissolve against him, as if the fight was melting right out of her. When he finally pulled away, she looked up at him, blinking dreamily and shivering at the same time.

He opened up his coat. "Come here."

She slid her hands beneath his sheepskin-lined coat and wound them around his back. He jumped a little when she pressed her cold palms to his back. She laughed softly and lay her head against his chest, and he closed his coat around her.

"Better?" he said, as the elevator slowly creaked its way to the third floor.

"Much," she said on a sigh.

She snuggled closer still, running her hands up and down his back. She exhaled, her breath warm against his chest. "Mmm. You feel *so* good."

He could have stood here forever, just like this, if it weren't for the fact that he was hot and hard and his jeans were growing more uncomfortable by the second and he wanted to make love to her right *now*.

The elevator ground to a halt and the doors opened. Wolfe pulled his keys out of his pocket. In his haste, he fumbled them a little, but managed to get the apartment door unlocked. Wendy slipped inside and headed straight to the bedroom.

By the time he had locked the door and followed her, he found her on the bed, wearing absolutely nothing. The sight of her sprawled out naked sent a jolt of desire tearing right through him.

He yanked off his jeans and boots, opened his dresser drawer, pulled out a condom and put it on. He lowered a knee between her legs and dropped his palms to her sides.

"It has to be now, sweetheart," he said. "And I mean *right now*."

She didn't say a word, just grabbed him by the shoulders and pulled him forward. He slipped into her, falling to his elbows at the same time. She wrapped her legs around him and he began to move inside her, deeper with every stroke, even as he fought to hold back. But she felt so hot and wet already, her inner muscles gripping him so tightly, that restraint was nearly impossible. Passion spiked inside him so quickly that he had to stop and drop his head against the bed to wait for the moment to pass. *Easy*, he told himself. *Easy...*

"Wolfe, please...oh, *please* don't stop."

Her words were little more than a plaintive moan, urging him on. To his surprise, the moment he gathered himself and thrust inside her again, she let out a strangled gasp and arched against him. For a split second she froze, her fingertips digging into his shoulders, and then a wild shudder of satisfaction rocked her entire body.

Astonished at the suddenness of her climax, Wolfe began to move in a hot, fierce rhythm, blinded by the feeling, plunging inside her as if he couldn't get enough, would never get enough. He couldn't remember a woman who had ever made him feel like this, who drove him crazy with need, who stripped away any pretense of control he might have had and drove him to a climax that stole his breath away.

Later, as he came back to earth again, he felt Wendy's hands on him, stroking his shoulders, his neck, his face, kissing him gently and whispering nothing words in his ear. He gathered her in his arms, and as he held her in the quiet darkness of his bedroom, her small body curled up next to his, he knew without a doubt that she'd stolen more than his breath away.

She'd taken his heart right along with it.

THE NEXT SUNDAY AFTERNOON, Wolfe and Wendy sat on the sofa, the paper scattered out on the coffee table. Wendy noticed that Wolfe picked up the Metro section first, while she always went for Texas Living. Not to be left out, Weenie jumped up on the table and spread his considerable bulk over the remainder of the paper. Consequently, when Wendy finished her section and exchanged it for the front page, she had to shove the cat aside to get to it. There had been a time when he would have hissed and fled, but now he merely gave her a go-to-hell look and reorganized himself into another goofy cat position.

After a while, Wendy stopped reading the paper and thumbed through the copies of *Entertainment Weekly* and *Premiere* she'd bought so she could keep up with what was going on in movies and TV. She'd called her agent a few times to insure he was still keeping her in mind. In the past five weeks, she'd managed to save almost fifteen hundred dollars now, so it wouldn't be long before she could be on the road to Los Angeles and back on track with her career.

But as the minutes passed, the strangest feeling came over her. She stopped reading. Lowered the magazine. Looked around her. Then she turned to Wolfe. After a moment he sensed her watching him and glanced up.

"What?"

She stared a moment more, then looked away. "Nothing."

No. Something. To her complete astonishment, she realized that even though she'd spent only a little over a month with Wolfe, this life felt normal. She was with a man who, at one time, she couldn't have fathomed having a civil conversation with, and here they were, lounging on the sofa, reading the Sunday paper together as if they'd been married for twenty years.

And sleeping together as if they were still on their honeymoon.

Wolfe looked back down at the newspaper. "Another

murder and two armed robberies. Not to mention all the break-ins. Will you look at these crime stats for the month? Good *God.*"

"I guess that eventually means more work for you, huh?"

Wolfe gave her a look of disgust. "I'd just as soon have to find another job for lack of work."

That reminded Wendy of something Ramona had told her, and she put down her magazine and moved closer to him, resting her arm along the back of the sofa. "Tell me about your brother."

"David?" He sounded surprised. "Not much to tell."

"Well, there is that story about how you came to work for Ramona."

Wolfe sighed. "Ramona has a big mouth."

Wendy rested her chin on her arm. "What was it like when you were growing up?"

He shrugged. "It wasn't bad when I was younger. The neighborhood was actually pretty nice."

"And when you got older?"

Wolfe kept looking at his newspaper, but she could tell he wasn't reading. "The older I got, the worse it got."

"How?"

Finally he let the paper fall to his lap. He just sat there a moment, as if he was thinking back, and when he spoke, his voice had a faraway quality to it.

"The storefronts gradually became abandoned. Drug dealers and prostitutes hung out on every street corner. Gangs ruled the neighborhood."

"If it was so bad there, why didn't you move somewhere else?"

"My mother wanted to. Believe me. But like most of the people in that neighborhood, she was so uneducated that she had a hard time finding a job that would even keep food on the table. Looking back, I suppose we were lucky to have a roof over our heads."

"And you were lucky to stay out of a gang."

"I refused to give in to that. But after that first time they cornered me, still I listened to it day in and day out. Blatant enticements sometimes, and other times taunts because I refused to listen to them."

"How did you deal with that?"

"Eventually I just learned to tune it all out. I didn't even hear the insults. I'd just stay in my own mind and keep on walking. It was the only way I could cope with it."

Wendy thought back to that first day when Wolfe had come into the office and Slade had been there. Slade had harassed him with one snotty comment after another, and it was as if Wolfe hadn't even heard him. Ramona had told her that someday she'd understand why.

Now she did.

"From the time I was ten or twelve years old," Wolfe said, "I went to sleep every night to the sound of gunfire in the neighborhood. I hated it. I used to bury my head under the pillow, but still I could hear it."

As if puzzle pieces were dropping into place, Wendy suddenly understood so much more about him than she ever had before. She remembered what Wolfe had told her after she'd screwed up Mendoza's apprehension and the man had pulled a gun. *I hate gunfire. Did I ever tell you how much I hate gunfire?*

She imagined the child he must have been, lying in bed, listening to his world crashing down around him and not being able to do anything about it.

"Then one day one of those bullets came through our window," Wolfe said. "The guy meant it for me. But David was the one who was hit."

"How bad was it?"

"An abdominal wound. I took him to the hospital. God, you should have seen the blood. I was never so scared in my life. And angry."

"That's when you took the law into your own hands."

"Yeah. I guess I did. That's when Ramona approached me about working for her. The money was better than what I could have made anywhere else."

Wendy nodded. "So David went to college, and you became a bounty hunter."

"Yes."

"College is expensive."

"Yes. But he got a scholarship. Like I said, he's the smart one."

"Did his scholarship cover everything?"

"Not everything."

"You paid the rest, didn't you?"

"He worked summers."

"And you paid the rest."

"Don't make me out to be some kind of hero, Wendy. It wasn't that much."

She doubted that. "I hope he appreciates what you did for him."

"He does."

"You're a good man."

"Tell that to the people I haul to jail."

"That's part of what makes you a good man."

She rubbed her fingertips up and down his arm. "And then David went on to get married. Have a family."

"Yes."

"Why do you live here?"

"What do you mean?"

"In this secluded place. I can't imagine why you'd want to hide yourself away like this."

"And I can't imagine why you'd want to go to Hollywood

and jump right into the limelight. All that glitz and glamour. It's bound to be crazy. And you'd have no privacy at all."

Wendy smiled. "Actually, to me it sounds exciting."

"And to me it sounds chaotic. I couldn't imagine living like that."

Chaotic. He'd used that word more than once to describe precisely the life he didn't want. Here, in this place, he'd found the peace and quiet he'd been denied for so long. He'd found a refuge from people who judged him on sight. But at what price?

He'd done everything he could to give his brother a nice life, yet he hadn't done the same for himself.

He's going to stay holed up in that weird apartment of his, Ramona had said, *and then one day he's going to turn around and wonder where his life went. And he's just too good a man for that.*

Ramona was so right. He needed more. He *deserved* more. Wendy realized that even though she and Wolfe spent almost every moment together when they weren't working, they did it mostly within the confines of this apartment.

"Let's go somewhere," Wendy said.

"Huh?"

"You don't get out much. Don't you ever get claustrophobic?"

"No. I get out all the time."

"I mean to someplace besides sleazy bars, the McDonald's drive-through and the county jail."

She sat up on the edge of the sofa, giving Weenie a shove so she could grab the movie section of the newspaper. She flipped through the pages.

"Oh, look! That new romantic comedy just opened. I'd love to see it."

"It'll be out on video soon."

"Video? I want to go to the theater."

Wolfe made a face.

"What's wrong with going to the theater?"

"Some moron always talks through the whole movie."

"But you can get movie popcorn. Far superior to micro-wave."

"I hate all those ads before the movie starts."

"Yeah, but there are trivia questions, too. I love those."

"Ticket prices are ridiculous."

"If we hurry, we can catch the last cheap show before five o'clock."

Wolfe sighed.

Wendy gave him a hopeful look.

Wolfe's expression twisted with disgust.

Impasse.

"We can sit in the back row and make out," Wendy said.

Dead silence. Slowly Wolfe lowered his newspaper and raised an eyebrow. "What time did you say it was playing?"

15

IT TURNED OUT TO BE a pretty good movie—what they saw of it, anyway. Fortunately it was a matinee, the theater wasn't full, and they had the back row to themselves, because even though Wendy hadn't actually been serious about making out in the back row, Wolfe was. By the time the credits rolled, she felt as if she were in high school all over again.

Yep. She'd have to rent the video.

As they were leaving the theater, Wendy ducked into the bathroom. Looking in the mirror, she saw that every bit of her lipstick had been kissed off. She smiled to herself, seriously considering going completely retro with the high-school behavior and enticing Wolfe into sex in the back seat of his SUV.

She came out of the bathroom to find the lobby far more crowded than it had been when they'd arrived at the theater. Wolfe was sitting on a bench waiting for her, leaning back against the wall, his arms folded over his chest. He wore his standard stony expression, which made him look like a sentry at the gates of hell. She smiled to herself, thinking it might be fun to sneak up on him and tickle him, just so he'd do the unthinkable and smile in public.

Just once. Just for fun.

Several feet away from him, two women stood talking, one of them holding a little girl who was about two years old. The child held a red rubber ball in her fist and squirmed in her mother's grip like every child on the planet who has been held too long and wants to cruise. The mother tussled with her for a moment more before finally giving up and putting her down. The moment she did, the child dropped the ball she'd been holding, and it rolled right between Wolfe's feet.

Wendy stopped and stood along the wall, watching as Wolfe leaned over and picked up the ball. The little girl spied her toy and toddled over. Wolfe held it up, drawing the child's attention, and she took it from between his fingers. Then she spied the cell phone he had clipped to his belt and pointed to it.

Wolfe unclipped it. He held it in front of her and pushed a few buttons. The phone rang. The little girl giggled, then reached for the phone herself. Wolfe held it out to her, pointing to the button for her to push. She did. When a different ring came out of it, she laughed again. Wolfe held the phone while she punched the button at least a dozen times and giggled with every ring.

Wendy smiled. There was something about the sight of her big, bad bounty hunter acting silly just to entertain a child that mesmerized her. And in that moment, she knew what a wonderful father he would be. Kind. Protective. Loving. The kind of man who would be totally devoted to his children and his family. Would she ever have guessed that the first night she met him? Was there any way she could deny it now?

Then she remembered Ramona's words. *Wolfe isn't close to many people in this world. But when he loves somebody, he loves them fiercely.*

Suddenly the strangest feeling came over Wendy. Her mind flashed forward to a possible future, images hitting her with the power of a hurricane-force wind. She and Wolfe. Living together. Loving together. Having children. Making a family. And all at once, she knew. For the many times she thought she'd been in love before, she couldn't possibly have been, because it had never, *ever* felt like this.

Love?

Oh, God. She was falling in love with him.

Wendy's knees suddenly felt weak, and she put her hand against the wall to steady herself. No. It couldn't be. How could she have known him for such a short time and feel this way?

Because he was so wonderful in so many ways that she couldn't even count them. He was the single most amazing package she'd ever unwrapped, peeling away his layers to find the real man beneath that gruff exterior.

But *love?*

The little girl finally toddled back to her mother's side, and Wendy walked over to where Wolfe sat.

He stood up. "Ready to go?"

"Yeah." She nodded toward the little girl. "Cute, huh?"

Wolfe smiled. "Yeah. She reminds me of one of David's kids."

Wendy looped her arm through Wolfe's as they walked out to the parking lot. All the way home, those feelings she'd had for him in the theatre lobby only grew stronger. And later that night, after they'd made love and she was lying in his arms, suddenly she couldn't bear the thought of leaving him. Los Angeles seemed fuzzy and distant, and her goal of stardom a pipe dream—something that thousands attempted but few achieved.

Was that what she really wanted?

The answer was yes. Of course it was. The very idea of giving up a dream that she'd held so close to her heart for the past several years was unthinkable. She couldn't let anything—or anyone—get in the way of that. Still, lying in Wolfe's arms like this, nothing about her life seemed as black-and-white as it had even two hours ago.

Fortunately, she didn't have to think about it now. It was going to take her at least several more weeks to get the money together she needed to leave for Los Angeles. Until that time came, she decided just to enjoy their time with each other and let the future take care of itself. But no matter what happened, she was always going to remember her detour through Dallas and the man who'd made her feel so wonderful, if only for a few brief moments of her life.

WOLFE SPENT most of Monday morning tracking down an alleged embezzler, who he finally discovered had faked an identity and was working at a new job in Fort Worth. He drove the fifty miles there, then waited for the guy to leave on a late lunch hour and picked him up without incident. He only wished all his apprehensions were that easy.

He drove back to Dallas, deposited the guy at the county jail, then headed to Lucky Bail Bonds to pick up a check. Afterward, because he was only a few blocks from Ramona's place, he decided to stop in there. For business reasons only, of course.

He found Ramona sitting at her desk, but Wendy was nowhere to be seen. Ramona nodded over her shoulder.

"She's in the back cleaning out the storeroom for me."

Wolfe stopped short. "Did I ask?"

"Oh, pardon me. My mistake. I thought all your gawking around the room for a certain little brunette actually meant something."

Wolfe wondered if he really was that transparent. The answer was probably yes.

He sat down beside Ramona's desk. "Anything new?"

She laid a file in front of him. "Wendy just got a line on this one for you. She did some calling around and found out from a next-door neighbor that this guy is holed up at his brother's house. He never leaves there. But this neighbor thinks he's alone during the day, so if you can get him out of the house, he's yours. Big bounty. Watch him, though. He's gonna be armed."

"Yeah," he said. "I know. The guy's got enough illegal-weapons charges against him to keep him in jail forever."

"Assuming he eventually ends up back in jail."

"Don't worry. I'll get him."

Just then Wendy poked her head out the door of the storeroom and gave Wolfe a big smile. "Wolfe! I thought I heard your voice. I've got a big box of printer paper in here I need to have moved. Would you mind?"

He got up and went into the storeroom. But the minute he came through the door, Wendy stepped from where she stood along the wall beside the door, grabbed him by his shirt collar and pulled him all the way inside the room. She backed against the copy machine and boosted herself up, grabbed his shirt again and hauled him between her knees. Wolfe caught the door with the heel of his boot and kicked it shut a second before Wendy's lips landed on his in a blistering kiss. At the same time, she circled her legs around him and pulled him right up against her with a little shimmy that woke up nerve endings he didn't even know he had.

When they finally came up for air, he gave her a look of sheer amazement. "You really are nuts. You know that?"

"Yeah. I know. Ever had sex on a copy machine?"

"Ramona would have us arrested. Capital offense."

"Okay. Then we'll just make out. I think that's only a misdemeanor."

God, he was crazy about this woman. Crazy about the way she talked to him, touched him, made love with him. She made him feel alive in a way he never had before. And when he started to think that maybe the copy machine looked pretty good after all, he knew he was going right off the deep end with her, and he didn't even mind taking the leap. At the very least, he decided he'd be the one to ambush her when she got home tonight and drag her straight to bed.

Suddenly the door swung open. Wendy jumped with surprise, dropping her legs from around his hips. Wolfe looked over to see Ramona standing there, her hand on the doorknob and her mouth twisted with disgust.

"Funny," she said. "I thought moving paper involved... paper."

"Ramona?" Wolfe said, turning back to Wendy and smiling furtively. "Don't you have something else you can be doing right now? Wendy and I are a little busy here."

"Well, let's see. Instead of coming into my own storeroom to get a printer cartridge so I can continue to run my own business, I suppose I could be telling my clerk that she's already had her coffee break for the afternoon and it's time to get back to work."

Wendy grinned. "Clerk? Does this mean I've been promoted from peon?"

The phone rang in the outer office, and Ramona gave Wendy a pointed stare.

"I'm on it, boss," Wendy said, hopping off the copy machine and scooting out the door.

Wolfe started to leave the storeroom. Ramona put her hand against his chest.

"Hold it, buster. I want to talk to you."

She pushed him back inside. She closed the door and leaned against it, staring at him with another one of those unreadable expressions that drove him crazy.

"Okay, Ramona," he said with a sigh. "What now? Am I going to get detention for making out under the bleachers?"

"Hell, no. I'm thrilled to death that you've finally figured out what to do with her."

Wolfe rolled his eyes.

Ramona folded her arms and took a few steps toward

him, her eyes softening. "I'm just hoping you've figured out a way to hang on to her."

Wolfe didn't want to be reminded of that. For every moment he was thinking about being with Wendy, another moment was spent thinking about her leaving.

"She's going to Los Angeles. It's just a matter of time."

"Maybe she'll change her mind about that."

"No. She'll never change her mind. You don't know what this means to her."

"What do *you* mean to her?"

It was a hell of a question. One he didn't have an answer to. "I'm not sure exactly."

"What does she mean to you?"

Wolfe looked away. He couldn't put that into words, either.

"Have you thought about telling her you're in love with her?"

Wolfe whipped around. "Hey, I never said—"

"You didn't have to. I see it in your eyes every time you look at her."

Ramona was right. She was so damned right that it killed him even to think about it. He was in love with Wendy. It was the word he'd been afraid even to think, but now he had to face it. Somewhere along the way she'd knocked down every defense he had and slipped deep inside him, shaking up his life in a way he'd never imagined. It wasn't just a matter of enjoying her company, or having somebody to talk to, or even great sex. She was the embodiment of every dream he'd ever had, every moment of his life when he'd dared to envision something other than his solitary existence.

"Maybe if she knew how you felt—"

"No," Wolfe said. "That wouldn't make a bit of difference. I'd just end up making a fool of myself."

"I don't think so. Tell her how you feel."

"I can't."

"You have to."

"I don't have to do a damned thing."

Ramona pointed her finger at him. "Don't you dare give up on this, Wolfe. She's the best thing that's ever happened to you. Don't you dare let her get away without so much as a—"

"Damn it, Ramona! Don't you think I want her to stay?"

Wolfe turned away, feeling out of control and hating it. Before Wendy had shown up in his life, nothing had ever made him lose his temper. But nothing had ever made him open up his heart, either. They were flip sides of the same coin—surges of emotion he'd never felt before—and he just didn't know how to deal with it.

"I've known from the beginning that this was only temporary," Wolfe said. "She's never even hinted at anything else. What makes you think she'd want to stay here?"

"Because she loves you."

Wolfe froze, the air between them quivering with words he couldn't fathom. "She told you that?"

"Not in so many words. But I can tell."

Wolfe let out the breath he'd been holding. In spite of Ramona's legendary intuition, he refused to believe what she was telling him. Couldn't make himself believe it.

"I didn't mean to jump all over you," Ramona said. "But if you let her leave, you're going to regret it for the rest of your life. And I care too much about you to see that happen."

He closed his eyes, knowing she was right.

"Wolfe," Ramona pleaded. "*Tell* her."

Maybe he could. Maybe tonight.

They were just going to have a quiet evening at home.

Maybe somehow he'd be able to work up the nerve, to find the words to tell her how he really felt.

The very thought of it terrified him.

But what if he said it, and she looked back at him with those beautiful brown eyes, that gorgeous smile, and somehow everything was as he'd always imagined it could be? Wasn't that worth the risk?

Suddenly he heard Wendy's voice. "Wolfe! Oh my God. *Wolfe!*"

She was calling his name so urgently that he turned and rushed out of the storeroom. As he entered the office, she spun around in her chair, her face full of excitement.

"You'll never guess what just happened!"

She leaped up and launched herself into his arms. Shocked, he held her for a moment, then set her back down on her feet. Her eyes were glowing with excitement.

"Wendy? What?"

"That was my agent on the phone. He's got an inside track about a new network television show about three kick-ass female private investigators. They want to cast a talented unknown in one of the lead roles. He sent over my head shots and my résumé, and the casting director says I've got exactly the look they want. I'm getting an audition!"

"An audition? In Hollywood?"

"Yes! This may be it. The break I've been waiting for!"

She fell into his arms again, hugging him tightly, her whole body quivering with excitement.

And Wolfe wanted to die.

16

WENDY WAS SO EXCITED she thought her heart was going to burst right out of her chest. A prime-time series. This could be it. The big one. The one that would propel her to stardom.

Wolfe pulled away and took her by the shoulders. "That's great, sweetheart. But I didn't think you were ready to go to Los Angeles yet. When do you have to be there?"

"They won't be casting for six weeks. Fortunately, my agent has some contacts, so he got an early heads-up. But I need to be there way sooner than that."

"Why is that?"

"My dark hair works for them. But there's a problem with the rest of me." She stared down at herself. "Let's just say that men don't watch this kind of series for the intellectual content."

Wolfe frowned. "Wendy, please tell me that you're not really going to have that surgery. Why aren't you just happy with yourself the way you are?"

"I *am* happy with myself. If not for my career, I wouldn't even think of doing it. It's just one of those sacrifices I know I have to make to get where I want to go."

Wolfe looked away, sighing with disgust.

"Look," she said. "I know you think it's not necessary, but my agent says it's a must. If I had anything at all, it might be different, but..." She looked at her chest again, shaking her head. "I'm going to be in competition with women with perfect bodies. I mean, *perfect*."

"Your body is perfect."

"To you, maybe, but not to the gazillion other men in America. So somehow I'm going to have to get the money to do it." She put her hand to her forehead and started to pace. "Okay. This isn't insurmountable. All I have to do is think a little. I've saved some money, but I still need..." She took a breath. "Oh, wow. At least four thousand dollars."

Damn. Why couldn't this have happened three months from now? If only she hadn't gotten stranded in Dallas, she'd be in Los Angeles right now, ready to follow the greatest opportunity she'd ever had in her life. Sometimes the brass ring came by only once. She had to grab it now. But how?

Then all at once she knew the solution.

She strode to Ramona's desk and dug through a stack of files, finally spying the one she wanted sitting out by itself. She yanked it up and flipped it open.

"Yes. This is it. This is how I can get the money." She glanced at Wolfe. "But I'm going to need your help."

"My help?"

"I did some calling around this afternoon and found out that this guy is hiding out in his brother's house, and he's always alone during the day. All we have to do is—"

"Whoa," Wolfe said suddenly. "Stop right there."

"What?"

"There is no 'we' here."

"Why not? I tracked him down, and I can help you lure him out. I'd say those things are worth you splitting the money with me, aren't they? And it's a big enough bounty to get me the amount I need."

"No way," Wolfe said, shaking his head. "You're not going anywhere near that guy."

She held up her hand. "Okay. I know why you're saying that. Because of the Mendoza thing. But I always learn from my mistakes. I won't screw it up, Wolfe. I'll do everything you say, when you say it. I swear I will."

"That has nothing to do with it."

"Then what?"

"Don't you get it? This guy isn't some shoplifter, or even a burglar. He's an arms dealer, probably in possession of every kind of illegal weapon known to mankind."

"It doesn't matter."

"What do you mean, it doesn't matter?"

"You'll be there. Just like last time. If something goes wrong—"

"If something goes wrong with a guy like that," he said sharply, "you could end up dead. And I care too much about you to let that happen."

I care about you.

Wendy froze, turning those words over in her mind. Every moment she'd spent with Wolfe over the past several weeks came back to her in a rush of emotion. She remembered how he'd picked her up off that street and kept her warm and safe. How he'd given her a place to stay. How he'd watched over her and protected her and made love to her in a way that no man ever had before. And how, every time their eyes met, he looked at her as if the sun rose and set for her and nobody else.

Then another image came to mind. She saw the factory where she'd worked. The gray walls. The pumping machinery. The hundreds of people lined up like robots, performing their mundane tasks. For four years she'd stood on that assembly line, and every day she'd experienced that same terrible feeling of obscurity, the one that had slithered inside her, wrapped itself around her lungs and squeezed the life out of her. The only thing that had saved her from going completely out of her mind was her dream of stardom, the dream she'd promised herself that someday she'd achieve.

"Wolfe, listen to me. This is a television series. *Prime time.* Do you know what the odds are of getting a break like this? I need that four thousand dollars!"

"Why? So you can screw up your body and eventually get your face on a few magazine covers? Don't you see how stupid that is?"

Stupid?

She felt as if he'd slapped her, and she recoiled for a moment until the sting subsided.

Then anger set in.

"So that's what this is really about, isn't it? It's not about the danger. It's about what I'm going to use the money for. You think my wanting to be an actress is stupid. You've always thought that. That's why you're refusing to help me."

"If it takes messing up your body to get what you want, then it isn't worth having."

"It *is* worth having! It's what I've wanted since I was eighteen years old!"

"Then go to Hollywood. Let some plastic surgeon change you into something you're not. But if you're willing to do something that drastic now, what will you be willing to do later when the next role comes along?"

"Whatever it takes. *That's* what I'm willing to do."

"God, Wendy! Can't you see what you're doing? You're chasing something that's never going to make you happy! So what if thousands of people adore you? At the end of the day when you go home alone, what difference does all that make?"

Wendy stared at him evenly. "You're a fine one to talk about going home alone."

Wolfe's jaw tightened. "I like my life the way it is. And I have no intention of changing it."

"Fine. You can waste your life away if you want to, but don't expect me to do the same."

Wolfe raised his chin, glaring at her, his body quivering with anger. And all at once it was as if she was looking at a stranger.

"I hope you get what you want, Wendy. And for your sake, I hope it really does makes you happy."

He turned and strode out the door, slamming it behind him. The impact rattled the door in its frame, the sound echoing through the office. After a moment, the echo died away, and silence filled the room.

Wendy bowed her head, suddenly feeling as if she was going to cry. The last thing she'd wanted was to fight with Wolfe.

"Just for the record," Ramona said, "Wolfe knows how important your acting career is to you."

She lifted her head. "He does?"

"Of course he does." Ramona paused. "More important to you than he is."

Wendy felt a pain in her chest that just might have been her heart breaking. "Don't do this to me, Ramona. Please don't lay a guilt trip on me. I care about Wolfe. You know I do. But if I don't find a way to do this now, I'll die wondering what might have been. And I just can't do that. I *can't*."

Just then the door opened. Wendy looked over to see Slade saunter into the office. Oh, *God*. She couldn't deal with him right now. She just couldn't.

"Hey," he said, nodding back over his shoulder. "I just saw Wolfe leaving. And boy, did he look pissed."

Ramona glared at him. "Beat it, Slade."

Slade looked back and forth between Ramona and Wendy, a sly smile playing over his lips. "Uh-oh. Something's up." He sat down in front of Wendy's desk. "Trouble in paradise?"

Wendy wondered if it would be a crime if she strangled somebody who really, truly deserved it. She thought maybe there had to be commendations for such things rather than prison sentences. Slade was an obnoxious, smart-mouthed, sexually fixated jerk who she truly wished would disappear from her life forever.

Then she had another thought.

He was also a bounty hunter.

She froze, turning that concept over in her mind. She thought her only chance of getting the money she needed to pursue her dream had walked out the door right along with Wolfe.

Maybe not.

"Slade," she said suddenly. "I need your help."

Ramona snapped to attention. "Wendy—don't even think it."

"Oh, yeah?" Slade said with an expression of sudden interest. "How's that?"

"I need four thousand dollars, and I need it now." She slapped the file down in front of him. "Arms dealer. I know where he is. I can lure him out. All I need is the muscle to take him down. We team up, split the bounty fifty-fifty. What do you say?"

Slade eyed her suspiciously. "Why aren't you asking Wolfe to help you?"

"None of your business. Will you do it or not?"

"Now wait a minute, Wendy," Ramona said. "You seem to be forgetting that I'm running the show here. It's my discretion whether to send somebody after that guy, and I'm choosing not to. Even if you pick him up, I'm not paying either one of you. Do you hear me?"

"Come on, Ramona!" Wendy said. "It's in your best interest if we get him. If you let him go, you'll have to forfeit the entire bond!"

"No, I won't. There's still time on this one. Wolfe will pick him up for me."

Wendy knew Ramona was right. *Damn.* What was she supposed to do now?

Slade sat back in his chair with a smug expression. "Don't worry, baby. It's not a problem. You need my help? I can help you."

Wendy sat up suddenly. "What do you mean?"

"Ramona's not the only bail bondsman in town, you know."

Ramona's eyes narrowed. "What the hell are you talking about?"

Slade looked at Wendy. "I've got a line on a high-end drug dealer for A1 Bail Bonds. Carl Braddock. An informant of mine spotted him at Red's. It's a crappy little sports bar where he's been the past two nights watching basketball playoffs. There's another game tonight. But he's always surrounded by his compadres, and they're not the kind of guys who go anywhere unarmed."

Wendy felt a stirring of hope. "If I can get him out of there alone, can you grab him?"

"Sure. Piece of cake."

"When do you think he'll be there tonight?" Wendy asked.

"Game starts at seven. You can start playing him right away, then move toward getting him out of there at halftime."

"Wendy," Ramona warned, "don't listen to him. It's too dangerous."

Wendy grabbed her purse from her desk drawer. She was going to need some new clothes for this, because she had no intention of going back to Wolfe's apartment. She checked her watch, then turned to Slade.

"I need something sexy to wear. Trinity River Thrift closes in half an hour, so we'd better move it."

As Wendy headed for the door, Ramona stood up.

"Wendy, if you walk out of here, I'm going to call Wolfe. I'm going to tell him what you're planning to do."

Wendy wondered what Wolfe would do if Ramona really did call him. He'd told Wendy he cared about her, and she knew it was the truth.

Maybe he even loved her.

But wasn't love all about supporting each other? Helping each other? Understanding each other? This had been her dream since she was eighteen years old. If he couldn't see how important it was to her, how could they ever hope to have a future together?

"It's getting late, baby," Slade said. "Are you with me, or not?"

She faced him. "Let's go."

Over Ramona's protests, Wendy walked out of the office and into Slade's car, pushing thoughts of Wolfe aside and concentrating only on the task ahead. This was her one chance, maybe her *only* chance, to make it really big.

And she wasn't going to pass it up.

WOLFE HAD PULLED OUT of Ramona's parking lot onto the street and started to drive, hitting the gas on the SUV hard, pushing the speed limit and not giving a damn. He didn't even know where he was going, but home wasn't an option. Going home meant sitting on his sofa in frozen silence. Staring at four walls. Having nothing but a scroungy cat for company. Looking at that rug and remembering.

So he just drove.

I like my life the way it is. And I have no intention of changing it.

That had been a lie. It had been such a big, fat lie that he'd barely been able to get the words out of his mouth. Now that he'd had a taste of just how wonderful life could be, he'd do anything to grab on to that feeling again. But Wendy had been the one to show him the way. And with her gone...

With her gone, nothing would ever be the same again.

Somehow he'd thought that if he loved her enough, she wouldn't let some surgeon mess with her like that and then put herself on display for some sleazy casting director who cared more about her body than anything else. But the minute—the second—somebody waved that opportunity in front of her, she'd leaped at it.

And she'd forgotten he even existed.

No. She hadn't forgotten. She wanted him to help her get four thousand dollars together. And as soon as that money was in her pocket, she'd have been out the door.

Then she would have forgotten him.

He wanted desperately to be angry about that. But the truth was that she'd never misled him. She'd never once suggested that she'd had even a random thought about staying in Dallas. He was the one who'd been a fool. He'd gone off in his own mind to that place where she'd throw away her ambition and stay with him forever. But that had been a fantasy—a fantasy that died instantly in the light of reality. Wendy was leaving, and she wasn't looking back.

His cell phone rang. He started to ignore it, but the incessant ring grated on his already irritated nerves. He unclipped it from his belt and looked at the caller ID.

Ramona.

No. No way could he talk to her right now. He didn't want her sympathy, he didn't want her advice, and with Ramona it was definitely going to be one of the two. Right now all he wanted was to be left alone. He punched a few buttons and turned off his cell phone, tossing it to the seat beside him.

He just wanted to be left alone.

WENDY SAT in Slade's car outside Red's, a painfully stripped-down bar and grille in a lousy part of town. A movable sign out front advertised basketball playoffs on big-screen TVs inside, along with price breaks on beer and margaritas.

Slade had told her that Braddock had enough money in his pocket that he could buy women the old-fashioned way—with drinks and dinner and assorted expensive gifts—so he probably wouldn't resort to hookers. So when Wendy picked up some clothes at Trinity River Thrift, she leaned toward skimpy without delving into sleazy. The bathroom had about half a roll of toilet paper, which now resided inside her brand-new thirty-eight double-D bra.

"Okay, baby," Slade said, as he killed the engine. "Do your stuff. Show him you're interested, offer him sex and get him out the door."

"So how are you and I going to talk to each other?"

"Huh?"

"Talk. You know. Communications. Listening devices. So you'll know what's going on inside."

Slade waved a hand. "Nah. That's not necessary. As long as you don't make the guy suspicious, you won't have anything to worry about."

Wendy felt a jolt of apprehension. She remembered how Wolfe had wired her to the max and given her every warning in the book about not taking any chances. And then he'd promised her he'd be in there in an instant if things went bad.

"What if I get into trouble?" Wendy said.

"Are you going to screw things up?"

"Well, no, but—"

"Then you won't get into any trouble. Now go. I'll be waiting to grab him the minute you come out."

Wendy paused, but Slade waved his hand at her, shooing

her out the door. She froze for a moment, all kinds of second thoughts pounding away at her, but then she decided that maybe Slade was right. As long as she didn't make a mistake—and she had no intention of doing that—everything was going to be just fine. And when it was all over with, she'd have money in her pocket and be on her way to Los Angeles.

She stepped out of the car into the cold night air and made her way across the gravel parking lot, tripping a little in her high heels. She opened the door and went inside. The bar was nothing more than a huge oblong room with big-screen TVs in every corner, the sound cranked up to supersonic levels so the crowd would hear it over their raucous cheering and groaning. Not surprisingly, the vast majority of the patrons were men and the vast majority of the waitresses had for real what Wendy had faked with Cottonelle.

She made her way to the bar and slid onto a bar stool, laying her coat and purse on the seat beside her. The bartender leaned over the counter and gave her a big grin.

"Basketball fan?" he said.

"Not really," she said, "but if you're looking for men, this is certainly the place to be, isn't it?"

"Smart woman. What'll you have?"

She ordered a gin and tonic, then sat back and surveyed the crowd. It took her a few minutes, but she finally spied Braddock sitting at a table with three other men. He was a well-built man in his forties, with sandy-brown hair, sharp features and a mug of beer in his hand. He wasn't exactly her idea of a high-level drug dealer, but then again, this wasn't a TV show, either.

Okay. She had her target. No problem. She could do this.

The bartender brought her drink. She picked it up, turned on her stool and zeroed in on Braddock. She had a good line of sight on him, and after a moment, he happened to glance at her. He started to look away, then did a double take, and she smiled at him. He stared at her for the count of three, then looked away again.

The game had begun. It was only a matter of time now.

WOLFE CAME UP the warehouse elevator, knowing he couldn't put off going home any longer. He hadn't seen his Porsche in the garage, but then he hadn't really expected to. After the argument he'd had with Wendy, he knew she wouldn't be coming home tonight. She was probably staying with Ramona. And in the end, that was probably a good thing. What else could they say to each other?

The moment he walked through the door, Weenie wound himself around his ankles. Wolfe went to the kitchen to feed him, then glanced over at his answering machine and saw the red light blinking. He thought about bypassing it, but at the last minute, flicked his finger against the button and heard Ramona's voice.

"Wolfe, there's trouble. You have to call me the second you get in. *Please.*"

Wolfe yanked up his cordless phone and dialed Ramona's number. She came on the line.

"Ramona. It's me. What's up?"

"It's Wendy."

Wolfe snapped to attention. "Wendy? What about her? What's wrong?"

"After you left the office, Slade came in. He has a line on a drug dealer with a big bounty from another bondsman. He's going to use Wendy as a lure. If they get him, Slade agreed to split the money with her."

"Who is this guy? How dangerous is he?"

"I don't know, exactly. But Slade said that he and his buddies would be armed to the teeth."

Wolfe's apprehension took a quantum leap. "When are they going after him?"

"Tonight. There's a crappy little bar where Slade says this guy and his buddies have shown up the past two nights to watch basketball playoffs. There's another game tonight at seven. Wendy's going in there to try to lure him out around halftime."

Wolfe checked his watch. Time was running out.

"What's the name of the place?"

"Red's."

Ramona gave him quick directions, and he wrote it all down on a pad by the phone, then ripped the sheet off and shoved it in his pocket. "I'm on my way right now."

"Keep me posted."

"I will."

Wolfe hung up the phone and ran into the other room, grabbing every bit of firepower he could conceivably carry, then went down the elevator and leaped into his car, berating himself the whole way.

Damn it, he should have helped her. Hell, he should have *given* her the money if that was what she wanted. Instead, she'd turned to Slade, a man who had only his own best interests at heart. He wouldn't watch out for her. He'd use her, but he wouldn't protect her, and as much of a maverick as he was, he could end up getting her hurt or killed.

And if anything happened to Wendy, Wolfe was never going to forgive himself.

17

FOR THE NEXT TWENTY MINUTES, Wendy pretended to watch the basketball game, keeping one eye on it and one eye on Braddock. If he looked her way, she held his gaze as long as she dared, and soon he was glancing her way more and more often. Then the halftime buzzer sounded. She saw him lean in to his buddies, say something, then rise from the table with his beer mug in hand.

He was heading her way.

Excitement surged through her. She'd done it. Now it was time to go in for the kill.

He slid onto the bar stool beside her, eying her up and down. "I'd ask if you come here often, but if you did, I guarantee you I would have remembered."

Wendy gave him a smile. "Is the game going your way?"

"Not tonight. I'm liable to walk away a little poorer than before."

"Then maybe you'd rather not put yourself through the misery of watching the second half."

"You have a better suggestion?"

"I was thinking maybe we could go someplace a little quieter." She raised an eyebrow. "My place, for instance."

He stared at her a long time without blinking. "Are you always this direct?"

She shrugged. "Well, I suppose we could sit here for another hour, you could buy me a drink or two, you could

watch your team lose, and *then* we could go to my place.''
She paused. ''Or we could just cut to the chase.''

His eyes narrowed with what looked like suspicion, and
for a moment she thought she'd pushed too hard too fast.
He glanced down at her artificially enhanced bustline, then
met her eyes again.

''Let's cut to the chase.''

Wendy felt a surge of exhilaration. She'd done it. He was
coming with her. In only a few minutes he'd be in handcuffs
and she'd be four thousand dollars richer.

''Let me just settle up with the bartender,'' she told him,
and reached into her purse for her wallet. When she flipped
it open, though, something fell out and fluttered to the floor.
She started to reach down to pick it up, but Braddock beat
her to it. And when he rose again and she saw what she'd
dropped, she felt a surge of panic.

It was one of Ramona's business cards.

Braddock looked at the card, then looked at Wendy. She
tried to stay calm and keep the guilty expression off her
face, but she knew she was failing miserably.

''Where did you get this card?'' he said.

She opened her mouth to respond, but absolutely nothing
came out.

''Is this a setup?''

''Setup?'' she said. ''What are you talking about?''

Braddock's eyes darted back and forth, as if he expected
to be ambushed at any moment. Then he rose from his seat
and clamped his hand onto her arm.

''Come on, baby. You and I are going somewhere to have
a little talk. And don't say a word on the way, or I'll make
sure it's the last one that comes out of your mouth.''

He dragged her by the arm through the bar, down a long
hall past the rest rooms and pay phones, then out the back
door of the bar. Her heart was beating in her chest like a bat-

tering ram, her breath coming in sharp little bursts. He spun her around and pinned her against the Dumpster.

"Tell me what's going on," he demanded. "Who's with you?"

The cold night air clogged Wendy's throat until it felt so tight that she couldn't have responded even if she wanted to.

Braddock looked nervously over his shoulder, then turned back to Wendy, his expression angry and impatient. "I asked you who's with you!"

"N-nobody's with me. I just came in here to have a drink. That's all."

Braddock leaned in close, stroked his hand down her hair, then very deliberately wrapped the length of it in his fist and pulled.

"I can make you talk, baby. And by the time I get finished, you'll be telling me the truth."

As HE DROVE to the bar, Wolfe gripped the steering wheel with a savage force, every nerve in his body tightened to the breaking point. Each time he missed a stoplight he cursed, then slammed his foot on the gas and burned rubber the second the light turned green.

Finally he spotted the place, a plain brick building with a half-lit neon sign out front. He pulled into the parking lot. As he was bringing his SUV to a halt, he spotted Slade's car, and his anger shot through the roof. The little bastard was kicked back in the driver's seat, his foot on the dashboard, tapping his fingertips on the steering wheel, just sitting there as if he had nothing better to do.

Wolfe got out of his car, slammed the door, stalked up to the driver's window and banged on it with his fist. Slade jumped halfway out of his skin, then rolled down the window.

"What's going on in that bar?" Wolfe demanded. "Where's Wendy?"

"What are you doing here?"

"Just answer me!"

"I don't know."

"What do you mean, you don't *know?*"

"She hasn't come out yet."

"Aren't you listening in?"

"Hell, no. It's a simple job. There's no need—"

"Why, you little—" Wolfe gritted his teeth and slammed his fist down on the roof of Slade's car. "*Damn* it!"

As Slade recoiled, Wolfe turned and strode toward the door of the bar.

"Hey! Where are you going?"

Wolfe didn't respond. A moment later he burst into the bar. The place was crowded. Televisions were blaring, and smoke filled the air. He walked through the room, looking for Wendy, intending to haul her right out the door the moment he found her.

She wasn't there.

Apprehension hit him like a thunderbolt. Could that guy have dragged her out of here when Slade wasn't paying attention?

The bathroom. Maybe she was in the bathroom.

Wolfe glanced around, finally spotting the hallway that led to the bathrooms and the pay phones. He shoved open the door to the women's bathroom and called out Wendy's name. Getting no response except the startled looks of the women lined up at the mirror, he spun around and started to head back up the hall. Then he noticed that the back door was ajar. He yanked it open.

Wendy. There she was.

He felt a swell of relief at seeing her, countered immediately by a rush of dread at the situation she was in. Braddock had her backed up against the Dumpster, her long hair wrapped around his fist. He looked angry. Wendy looked terrified. A burn of anger ignited inside Wolfe, then exploded him into action.

WHEN WENDY SAW WOLFE standing in the doorway, she couldn't believe her eyes. But then he strode outside, looking as big and bad as she'd ever seen him before, a huge, menacing presence that made Braddock's eyes go wide as searchlights. Wolfe really was here. He really was angry.

And he really was going after Braddock.

As Wolfe stalked toward him, Braddock instantly made the connection. He pulled a gun from beneath his coat, tightened his fist around Wendy's hair and yanked her closer. But when he moved the weapon up to point it at her head, he was a second too late. Wolfe swung his arm out and punched Braddock in the face. The gun went flying, crashing into the Dumpster with a loud clatter.

The second Wendy felt Braddock's grip loosen, she scrambled away, and Wolfe was on him in an instant. He grabbed him by the collar, spun him around and forced him down to the ground. Once Braddock's nose was in the dirt, Wolfe put a knee against the small of his back, hauled his hands behind him and clipped on a pair of handcuffs.

Breathing hard, Wolfe rose to his feet and turned to Wendy, standing tall, his breath clouding the air, every inch a man in control, a man who protected those he loved, a man who had stood between her and disaster one more time. And just the sight of him made her want to cry with relief.

He held out his hand. She took three steps forward and fell into his arms.

"Wolfe," she said. "You're here. You came. Oh, God, I can't believe you came."

"Are you okay, sweetheart? Did he hurt you? I swear to God I'll kill him if he hurt you."

"No. No, I'm fine. I'm just..." She began to cry, sobs choking her voice to the point that she could barely speak.

"It's okay," he said, holding her tightly. "Everything's okay."

"It was so stupid of me," she said. "I never should have done this. Never. I'm sorry...I'm so sorry..."

"Let's get out of here."

"Braddock—"

"We'll let the cops pick him up."

Wolfe took off his coat and put it around Wendy's shoulders, then dialed 911 on his cell phone and explained the situation. Leaving Braddock squirming on the ground, he put his arm around Wendy and led her toward his car. A police car soon came down the street, followed shortly by another one. After they pulled into the parking lot, Wolfe signaled to the two officers and told them where Braddock was.

As the officers headed around the building to pick him up, Wolfe opened the car door for Wendy and she slid into the passenger seat. He put one arm along the top of the window and the other on the roof of the car and leaned in to talk to her.

"Are you sure you're okay?"

She breathed deeply. "Yeah. I'm fine."

Then Wolfe glanced across the front seat out the driver's window, and his expression turned grim. Wendy looked over to see Slade approaching the car.

"Sweetheart?" Wolfe said. "Will you excuse me for just a minute?"

"Sure."

He closed the car door, circled the front of the vehicle and walked toward Slade, who saw Wolfe coming, but froze like a deer in the headlights. Wolfe took a double handful of his coat collar, turned and slammed him up against the driver's door of the SUV. Even though the windows of the car were up, Wendy could hear every angry word he spoke.

"You little bastard! How in the hell could you let her go in there like that? *How?*"

"Hey, she was the one who wanted to do it!"

"While you sat out here in the parking lot without a clue what was going on? Do you know how close she came to getting hurt?"

"Hey, man, it was just one of those things, you know? I didn't—"

"Shut up," Wolfe growled, slamming him against the car again. "I don't want to see you come near Wendy again. Ever. If I do, I'm going to start pounding. And I'm not going to stop pounding until there's nothing left of you. Do you understand?"

Slade nodded. Wolfe slung him sideways. He stumbled a little, then came to his feet.

"Now, get the hell out of here!"

Slade lurched away, and Wolfe stood watching until he got into his car and disappeared out of the parking lot.

Wendy sat in the car, amazed at what she'd just seen. After all the snide comments Slade had made toward Wolfe over the years, the only thing that had made Wolfe lose his temper and go after Slade was the fact that he'd come so close to hurting her. And she loved him for it.

Wolfe got into the car beside Wendy, his face still clenched with anger. He put his hands on the steering wheel, took a deep breath and let it out slowly.

"Wolfe," she said, "I'm so sorry about this. For dragging you out here and putting you in danger, too. And I'm sorry about the fight we had. Every single time I've needed you, you've been there." Tears filled her eyes. "I appreciate that. You don't know how much."

For a long time he just stared ahead, his fingers clenching the steering wheel. "Los Angeles..."

"No." Wendy closed her eyes. "Please don't talk about that now."

"You're still leaving."

He spoke it as a statement, not a question. But all at once, Wendy had the terrible feeling that in order to get that one thing in her life she desperately wanted, she was going to have to give up something even more precious.

She couldn't believe this. Before she'd gotten waylaid in Dallas, she never would have thought that anything could deter her from her dreams of stardom. But now...

"I don't know what I'm going to do," she told him.

He nodded, still refusing to meet her eyes. "What about tonight? Where do you want me to take you?"

Wendy didn't know what was going to happen tomorrow. She only knew where she wanted to be tonight. "I want to go home," she said softly. "With you."

Several more seconds passed. She had the most uncanny sensation of her dream fading away, until all she could think about was Wolfe taking her into his arms and telling her he wanted to make love to her, just as he'd done so many times before.

To her dismay, though, he merely nodded. Without saying another word, he started the car and headed toward his apartment.

WHEN WOLFE AND WENDY GOT HOME, she slipped her arms around his neck and kissed him. For a moment he felt a rush of optimism that maybe she'd changed her mind and was going to stay. But he knew that wasn't necessarily true, and believing it would only make things more difficult later if she really did say goodbye.

This had been a mistake. He should have taken her to stay

with Ramona, because if he made love to her tonight and she left him tomorrow, he wasn't sure he'd ever recover. He gently pushed her away, using up every bit of willpower he had. Consequently, when she reached for him a second time, he had no resolve left with which to fight.

Flooded by a sudden surge of passion, he groaned with resignation, tangled his fingers in her hair and kissed her deeply, then swept her into his arms and took her to his bedroom. Lord, how he wanted her, even if it was for the last time.

Especially if it was for the last time.

Afterward, they lay in silence for a long time, their bodies twined together, but the more time that passed, the more restless Wolfe became. Thoughts kept pounding at his mind that wouldn't go away, and he knew that sooner or later there was something he had to do.

He tossed the covers back and rose from the bed.

"Where are you going?" she asked.

"I'll be back in a minute."

He went into the other room. A few moments later he came back and sat down on the bed beside her. He flipped on the lamp and handed her a piece of paper.

"What's this?" she asked.

"A check for five thousand dollars."

Wendy stared at it with disbelief. "What?"

"It's the four thousand you need, plus another thousand to make things easier."

"But...but why?"

"Because all this has made me realize just how important your dream is to you, and I want to help you make it come true."

Wendy stared at him incredulously.

"Take this money and do whatever you think you have to do with it. I mean that. But Wendy..." He bowed his head for a moment, silenced by a swell of emotion. Then he looked at her again. "I just want you to know that you'll always be beautiful to me just the way you are. I love you no matter what. And I always will."

Wendy stared at him, tears filling her eyes, then looked back down at the check. "I can't take this."

"Yes. I want you to have it."

"No. I'm not going to Los Angeles. I can't leave here if it means losing you."

Wolfe's heart skipped with hope, but just as quickly he buried the feeling, refusing to let it sway him. "No, Wendy. Don't say that. It's nothing but gratitude talking."

"No. It's not gratitude. It's love."

Love.

Wolfe wanted to believe that. He wanted to believe it so much that he almost took Wendy into his arms again so he could keep her right here with him, both of them sequestered from the rest of the world forever. But he knew he couldn't do that. Not when she wanted something so desperately that he could never hope to give her.

He smoothed his hand down her arm and took her hand in his. "Wendy, listen to me. If you don't do this, you'll spend the rest of your life wondering what might have been. And you'll hate me for being the one who kept you from it."

"It's my decision. I want to stay right here."

"No. You're going to Los Angeles. And you're going to be a big success. And in the meantime, I'm going to get subscriptions to *Entertainment Weekly* and *People*."

"Subscriptions?"

"Yeah. I want to be sure I don't miss your face on the cover."

Wendy stared at him, her expression growing shaky. She opened her mouth to speak, but then her face crumpled and she began to cry. He pulled her into his arms, hugging her fiercely, feeling as if his heart was breaking. He couldn't even imagine what life was going to be like without her.

Yes, he could. It was going to be just as cold and empty as it had been before she'd come. And he couldn't bear the thought of it.

"I'm going to miss you so much," he whispered.

He held her for a long time, rocking her gently, letting her cry, cherishing every moment because there were so few of them left. Slowly her tears subsided. Then she pulled away and looked at him, and her face suddenly brightened.

"No," she said. "You're not going to miss me."

"What?"

"You're coming with me."

Wolfe blinked with surprise. "To Los Angeles?"

"Yes."

"I can't do that."

"You can't?"

"No. I can't leave here."

"Why not?"

Why not?

Wolfe opened his mouth to answer, then realized he didn't have a damned thing to say in response. Absolutely nothing. He had no life here. Wendy had been right about that. He hadn't had any life at all until she showed up.

Now she was his life.

Realization slowly crept in, making him see himself more clearly than he ever had before. For years he'd stayed holed up in this warehouse apartment, seeking solitude, hiding from the ugliness of his past, hiding from the dreams he'd always had of having a wife and a family because he saw no way of them ever coming true.

Now he saw a way.

"I can't guarantee you what it'll be like," Wendy said. "I've heard Los Angeles can be a crazy place. It's more expensive to live there, so God only knows what kind of apartment we'll be able to get. It'll probably be pure chaos until we get settled, and I know you don't like that, but—''

"When do we need to be there?"

Wendy blinked. "Did you say 'we'?"

"I said 'we.'"

"Does this mean you'll come with me?"

"I'll go anywhere on the planet, Wendy. As long as I'm with you."

"Oh, Wolfe..." She threw her arms around him, hugging him with such excitement that she practically knocked him over backward. Then she stopped short.

"But what will you do there?" she asked.

"There are criminals in every big city. Some of them even jump bail."

Wendy smiled. "I guess that's right."

"But that isn't the only option I've got. I'm thinking maybe I need to make a change. Get into another line of work. Maybe this is the way to make that happen."

Wendy took his face in her hands and kissed him, her expression positively ecstatic. "Yes," she said. "Whatever you want. And I'll help you any way I can."

He thought about what lay ahead. He thought about trading his methodical, predictable, secluded life for the unknown. Living in an unfamiliar place. Stepping out into the world. But to his surprise, he didn't feel the least bit apprehensive. Instead, excitement surged inside him.

"Now, this may be a pipe dream for me," Wendy said. "I mean, I could get there and they could decide I'm all wrong for the part. I may have to take stupid jobs for years before anybody even notices me. Or maybe I'll never make it at all. I may end up falling flat on my face, and all of this will have been for nothing."

He stared down at her, brushing a strand of that gorgeous

dark hair away from her temple. "It doesn't matter if you fall," he said. "I'll be there to catch you."

Her eyes instantly filled with tears again, but they were good tears, the kind that meant he was finally going to have the kind of life he'd always dreamed about with a woman he would love forever. He'd finally come out of the darkness and into the light, and it was Wendy who'd taken him there.

Epilogue

EVENING SUN STREAKED through the windows of the warehouse loft, lighting the living room with a pale rosy glow. Wendy sat on the sofa reading a magazine, Weenie curled up next to her, his head resting against her thigh. A candle burned on the coffee table, giving off the pale scent of warm vanilla, and the relaxing sound of soft jazz drifted through the air.

She glanced at her watch. It was getting late.

She looked out the window. The summer sunset bathed the cityscape of Los Angeles in warm hues of red and orange, and beyond that, the ocean glistened like a new copper penny. It was growing too dark to read, so she reached up and flipped on the floor lamp beside the sofa, then checked her watch again.

Where *was* he?

Finally she heard a key in the lock. The door opened, and Wolfe came into the apartment. She rose from the sofa, dislodging Weenie's head from her leg. The cat merely rearranged himself and closed his eyes again.

Wendy laid the magazine she'd been reading on the coffee table, then slid into Wolfe's arms.

"It's about time you got home," she said. "How was your day?"

"Couldn't have been better."

"The interviews went well?"

"I hired both men. One's an ex-cop, the other ex-military.

They know about weapons, evasive driving, threat assessment, and both of them have worked as bodyguards. They're just the kind of guys I'm looking for."

What had started as an inkling of an idea on their drive from Dallas a few months ago was slowly becoming a reality. In Los Angeles, there was no shortage of high-profile social events, visiting foreign dignitaries and celebrities, all of whom needed security. With the commitment Wolfe was showing toward his new business, Wendy had no doubt that within a few years, Wolfe Security Services would be the most sought-after security company in town.

She took him by the hand. "Come here. I have something to show you."

She sat him down on the sofa, then handed him the *Entertainment Weekly* she'd been reading, which had a cover story about a hot new series in the works starring three beautiful kick-ass private investigators.

One of them was Wendy Wolfe.

"The magazine's out already?" Wolfe said. "I didn't think it was going to be on the stands for another week."

"Subscription copies come early. It was in the mailbox when I got home. So what do you think?"

He stared at the cover, then looked up at Wendy, a warm smile lighting his face. "I think," he said softly, "that you're going to be a star."

Wendy felt a surge of pure happiness. This was it. This was the thing she'd thought about all those years in Glenover, Iowa, when she'd felt herself melting into obscurity and dreamed of the day she'd be on the cover of a magazine like this.

Then Wolfe's smile faded. "Hold on. There's a problem here."

"What's the matter?"

"One look at this photo, and every man in America is going to be lusting after you."

Wendy grinned. "Nah. My co-stars are the ones with the big boobs. They're the ones the men will be looking at."

"Not when you're the prettiest of the three."

Wendy snuggled up next to him. "They can look all they want to. You're the only one who gets to touch."

"Damn right."

Wolfe tossed the magazine to the table, then dragged her into his arms and kissed her. One thing led to another, and soon she was lying naked on the fluffy beige-and-green rug from Trinity River Thrift Store, the one she didn't have the heart to get rid of no matter how big her paycheck was now. Wolfe lay beside her, staring at her with that expression she'd grown to love so much, the one that said the very air she breathed was sacred to him.

Wendy had reached her dream. And somehow she knew that as the years passed, it was going to be everything she'd imagined it would be. But as much as she loved the spotlight, she already knew that the adoration of millions wasn't going to compare to the love she saw in this one man's eyes.

Live the emotion

INDECENT *by Tori Carrington*

Sleeping with Secrets
From the moment Lucky Clayborn struts into his
office, psychologist Colin McKenna wants the fiery
redhead badly. But how can he possibly have a
proper patient/doctor relationship—something his
career depends upon—when all he wants to do is to
get lucky…with Lucky?

WICKED GAMES *by Alison Kent*

www.girl-gear…
gIRL-gEAR VP Kinsey Gray is not happy to hear
Doug Storey is moving. She and the sexy architect
have some history, but Kinsey was never quite sure
how she felt about him. Now that he's leaving, it's
time she made up her mind. With the help of a
three-step plan to seduce Doug, Kinsey's positive
she'll persuade him to stay.

Don't miss out!
These sexy reads are on sale from
4th March 2005

*Available at most branches of WHSmith, Tesco, ASDA, Martins,
Borders, Eason, Sainsbury's and all good paperback bookshops.*

Visit www.millsandboon.co.uk

Published 18th March 2005

New York Times Bestselling Author

Jennifer Crusie

Charlie All Night

"Crusie has a gift for concocting nutty scenarios
and witty one-liners..." —*People* magazine

M404

WIN a romantic weekend in PARiS

To celebrate Valentine's Day we are offering you the chance to WIN one of 3 romantic weekend breaks to Paris.

Imagine you're in Paris; strolling down the Champs Elysées, pottering through the Latin Quarter or taking an evening cruise down the Seine. Whatever your mood, Paris has something to offer everyone.

For your chance to make this dream a reality simply enter this prize draw by filling in the entry form below:

Name _____

Address _____

_____ Tel no: _____

Closing date for entries is 30th June 2005

Please send your entry to:

Valentine's Day Prize Draw
PO Box 676, Richmond, Surrey, TW9 1WU